Robin's Diary

Robin's Diary

Judith Pinsker

Based on the story by Claire Labine

Selections from Stone's Memory Book by Claire Labine
Foreword by Kimberly McCullough

**daytime
press**

Distributed by Chilton Book Company, Radnor, Pennsylvania

Manufactured in the United States of America

Produced by March Tenth, Inc.
Graphic art and interior design by Paul Leibow

Cover design by Anthony Jacobson
Cover photo by Mark Jenkins
Snapshot used on cover by Cathy Blaivas

Photos on pages 104, 105, 108, 111, 112, and 113 by Cathy Blaivas / ABC
Photo on page 145 by Jim Ober / ABC
Photos on pages 12, 41, 43, 49, 127, 150, and 166 by Craig Sjodin / ABC
Photos on pages 94 and 95 by Donna Svennevik / ABC
Photo on page 29 by Vivian Zink / ABC

ISBN 0-8019-8775-X

A Cataloging-in-Publication record for this book is available from the Library of Congress.

4 5 6 7 8 9 0   4 3 2 1 0 9 8 7 6 5

Acknowledgments

My most profound thanks go to Claire Labine, mentor and friend, for bringing such dimension and truth to Robin Scorpio and Stone Cates and for trusting me with their story. Also for editorial guidance throughout, for general help and encouragement over the years, and for taking a chance on a new writer a long time ago.

I also want to thank my husband, Adam, and my son, Joel, for love and support through an emotionally demanding time, as well as for reviewing and commenting on the manuscript. Thanks also to my agent, Leo Bookman, for his continued encouragement and support; to Egon Dumler for helpful legal counsel; to Erica Gilles for reading and commenting; and to the R&SDL online chat group, who helped without knowing it.

Claire and I would like to thank Wendy Riche, Executive Producer of *General Hospital*, for her leadership and vision, and Francesca James, Supervising Producer, Julie Carruthers, Producer, and Shelley Curtis, Consulting Producer, who together orchestrate the large and talented team that daily keeps *General Hospital* at an extraordinary level of achievement. We would mention them all by name if there were space, but we thank each one of them sincerely.

We do want to acknowledge the particular contributions of:

—Our colleagues on the *GH* writing team: Matthew Labine, Eleanor Mancusi, Meg Bennett, Ralph Ellis, Michel Val Jean, Lewis Arlt, Stephanie Braxton, Karen Harris — all of whose creativity is drawn upon in these pages.

—Kimberly McCullough, Michael Sutton, and John J. York, the actors who bring Robin, Stone, and Mac to life so brilliantly, as well as the entire *GH* cast, who make our friends in Port Charles incredibly real for us, with a special note of thanks to Lee Mathis, as Jon Hanley.

—Elizabeth Korte, Script Continuity, whose encyclopedic knowledge of *GH* history was invaluable and who took on a lot of extra work very cheerfully, as did Claire's assistant, the amazing Jane Greenstein, and writers' assistants Davis Goldschmid, George Doty, IV, Marc Dabrusin, and Jim Morgan.

At ABC our sincere thanks go to: Pat Fili-Krushel, Maxine Levinson, Cody Dalton, Angela Shapiro, Regina DiMartino, Maria Melin, and Jill Yager, and most especially to:

Barbara Bloom, Director of Daytime Programming, West Coast, who had the idea for *Robin's Diary* and saw it through.

At Chilton Book Company our thanks go to Chris Kuppig, for his enthusiastic commitment to and management of the project, and to Susan Keller, without whose energy, editing skill, diplomacy, and general midwifing, this book couldn't have happened. Also to Sandra Choron and Paul Leibow, who did the impossible on a more than tight schedule.

Our thanks, too, to the people and organizations who aided us in research: Dr. Steven Miles, UCLA Center for Clinical AIDS Research; Martha Aleman, Outreach Coordinator, Adolescent AIDS Program of Montefiore Medical Center; Gay Men's Health Crisis, Inc; and the Centers for Disease Control.

—Judith Pinsker

Judy Pinsker's work has, as usual, left me in a state of delighted admiration and awe.

"Based on the story by Claire Labine," which suggests that I'm the sole source of the original material, is woefully inaccurate. Matt Labine, Eleanor Mancusi, and I laid out the story of Robin and Stone, as we did the other stories on *General Hospital* for the past two years. The talents and sensibilities of each member of the writing team enhanced and illuminated it. I am so grateful to the writers of *General Hospital*. I am proud to work with them.

Judy has thanked many people for their help to us, but I need to repeat: To Wendy Riche for her joy and guidance, to Barbara Bloom f or all her insights, to Francesca James, Julie Carruthers, and Shelley Curtis for their production wizardry, and to Pat Fili-Krushel and Maxine Levinson for unprecedented support and stalwart faith . . . love and thanks always.

And to the actors, our hearts.

—Claire Labine

Foreword

The story of Robin and Stone is a love story. It's about the love that Robin and Stone share, and it's about the love they inspire around them.

Personally I have been inspired by the people with HIV or AIDS that were kind and courageous enough to share their lives with me as I prepared to tell this story. Their compassion, their selflessness, their sense of humor in the face of this disease, and the prejudice that surrounds it, have been incredible.

It is my wish that everyone who reads this book will think a little differently about people with HIV or AIDS, will educate themselves about the disease, and will reach out a little more and be afraid a lot less.

I hope you enjoy Robin and Stone's story, and I hope you will think about just how powerful love can be.

Kimberly McCullough
Robin Scorpio, of ABC Daytime's *General Hospital*

ABC Daytime is proud to donate its portion of the proceeds from *Robin's Diary* to AIDS-related organizations.

Robin's Friends and Acquaintances in Port Charles

RUBY ANDERSON   Owner of Kelly's diner; aunt of Luke Spencer and Bobbie Jones.

NED ASHTON   Grandson of Edward Quartermaine; son of Tracy Quartermaine; CEO of ELQ Industries, a Fortune 500 corporation owned by the Quartermaine family; L&B Music recording artist and lead singer of Idle Rich rock group, using stage name Eddie Maine; love interest and later husband of Lois Cerullo.

BRENDA BARRETT   Close friend of Robin; partner with Lois Cerullo and Sonny Corinthos in L&B Music, a recording company; "Face of Deception" model representing Deception cosmetics; love interest of Sonny Corinthos.

KATHERINE BELL   Former con artist; public relations specialist; frequent love interest and scam partner of Damian Smith.

EMILY BOWEN   Young daughter of Monica Quartermaine's friend Page Bowen; lives with Monica and Alan Quartermaine after her mother's death.

GINA CATES   Younger sister of Stone and Jagger Cates; adopted by wealthy parents after the breakup of the Cates family.

JAGGER CATES   Older brother of Stone and Gina Cates; in an effort to reunite his broken family, hired Mac Scorpio to locate Stone and Gina; eventual husband of Karen Wexler Cates, a close friend of Robin.

MICHAEL "STONE" CATES   Love of Robin's life; high school dropout and former runaway; brother of Jagger and Gina Cates; taken off the streets and given food, shelter, and a job by Sonny Corinthos.

LOIS CERULLO   Rock music promoter who moved to Port Charles from Brooklyn; childhood friend of Sonny Corinthos; partner with Brenda Barrett and Sonny Corinthos in L&B Music; love interest and later wife of Ned Ashton.

RYAN CHAMBERLAIN   Serial killer; former General Hospital pediatrician who seeks revenge on his twin brother, Kevin Collins.

LUCY COE   President of Deception Cosmetics; love interest of Kevin Collins.

KEVIN COLLINS General Hospital psychiatrist; twin brother of Ryan Chamberlain; love interest of Lucy Coe.

MIKE CORBIN Maitre d' at Luke's, Luke Spencer's blues nightclub; estranged father of Sonny Corinthos.

SONNY CORINTHOS Partner with Lois Cerullo and Brenda Barrett in L&B Music; partner with Luke Spencer in Luke's; love interest of Brenda Barrett; unofficial big brother of Stone Cates; suspected of ties to organized crime.

SEAN DONELY One of Robin's godfathers; Chief of Port Charles Police; husband of Tiffany Hill; former head of the World Security Bureau (WSB) intelligence agency.

JENNY ECKERT Distant cousin of Luke Spencer; former wife of Ned Ashton; love interest of Paul Hornsby.

JON HANLEY AIDS patient and activist.

AUDREY HARDY General Hospital's Head of Nursing; wife of Steve Hardy; mother of Tom Hardy.

SIMONE HARDY General Hospital pediatrician; estranged wife of Tom Hardy; love interest of Justus Ward.

STEVE HARDY General Hospital's Chief of Staff; husband of Audre Hardy; father of Tom Hardy.

TOM HARDY General Hospital psychiatrist; son of Steve and Audrey Hardy; estranged husband of Simone Hardy.

TIFFANY HILL Former B-movie actress; TV news reporter and owner of WLPC TV station; wife of Sean Donely; close friend of Robin.

PAUL HORNSBY Former husband of Tracy Quartermaine; love interest of Jenny Eckert.

BOBBIE JONES General Hospital's Chief Surgical Nurse; wife of Tony Jones; stepmother of daughter B.J. Jones; adoptive mother of Lucas Jones; sister of Luke Spencer; niece of Ruby Anderson.

FELICIA JONES Fiancee of Mac Scorpio, as well as co-owner with him of Outback restaurant and partner with him in Jones and Scorpio, Private Investigators; twice married to and divorced from Frisco Jones; mother of two daughters by Frisco: Maxie and Georgie Jones.

FRISCO JONES One of Robin's godfathers; close friend of Robert and Anna Scorpio; brother of Tony Jones; twice married to and divorced from Felicia Jones; father of Maxie and Georgie Jones.

TONY JONES General Hospital neurosurgeon; father of daughter B.J. Jones; adoptive father of Lucas Jones; brother of Frisco Jones; husband of Bobbie Jones.

DUKE LAVERY Robin's deceased stepfather who had ties to organized crime.

MIGUEL MOREZ Singer from Puerto Rico; L&B recording artist; bartender at the Outback restaurant; love interest of Lily Rivera.

ALAN QUARTERMAINE General Hospital's Assistant Chief of Staff; husband of Monica Quartermaine; father of A.J. and Jason Quartermaine.

ALAN QUARTERMAINE, JR. (A.J.) Son of Alan and Monica Quartermaine; older half-brother of Jason Quartermaine; recovering alcoholic; head of Charles Street Development Foundation (CSF), a nonprofit organization established by the Quartermaine family to aid development of small businesses in the Charles Street area.

EDWARD QUARTERMAINE Patriarch of Port Charles' most illustrious family; Chairman of the Board of ELQ Industries; father of Alan and Tracy Quartermaine and Bradley Ward; husband of Lila Quartermaine.

JASON QUARTERMAINE Son of Alan Quartermaine and adoptive son of Monica Quartermaine; social activist; premed student; Charles Street Foundation board member; love interest of Keesha Ward.

MONICA QUARTERMAINE Renowned General Hospital heart surgeon; member of ELQ Industries board; husband of Alan Quartermaine; mother of A.J. Quartermaine; adoptive mother of Jason Quartermaine.

LILY RIVERA Estranged daughter of a Puerto Rican organized crime boss; close friend of Sonny Corinthos; love interest of Miguel Morez.

MAC SCORPIO Robin's uncle and legal guardian; brother of the late Robert Scorpio; fiancee of Felicia Jones, as well as co-owner with her of Outback restaurant and partner with her in Jones and Scorpio, Private Investigators.

ROBERT AND ANNA SCORPIO Robin's deceased parents; World Security Bureau agents; Robert had no knowledge of Robin until she was 7 years old; Anna and Robert remarried for a brief time before both were killed.

JOE SCULLY Mentor to Sonny Corinthos; alleged organized crime figure.

SIGMUND Pet duck of Lucy Coe.

HARRY SILVER Assistant to Sonny Corinthos in all "unofficial" business.

DAMIAN SMITH Son of deceased organized crime boss Frank Smith; frequent love interest and scam partner of Katherine Bell.

FILOMENA SOLTINI Robin's "Grandma Fil"; a friend of Anna Scorpio entrusted to raise Robin up to age 7.

LAURA SPENCER Community activist; social work student; wife of Luke Spencer; mother of Lucky and Lesley Lu Spencer.

LUKE SPENCER Best friend of Robin's father, Robert Scorpio; owner of Luke's, a blues nightclub; husband of Laura Spencer; father of Lucky and Lesley Lu Spencer.

JUSTUS WARD Attorney and Port Charles City Council member; Charles Street Foundation board member; love interest of Simone Hardy; son of Bradley Ward; grandson of Mary Mae Ward.

KEESHA WARD College student; assistant to A.J. Quartermaine at Charles Street Foundation; love interest of Jason Quartermaine; daughter of David Ward; granddaughter of Mary Mae Ward.

MARY MAE WARD Operates Bradley Ward House for foster and HIV+ children; mother of Bradley, David, and Idys Ward; grandmother of Justus and Keesha Ward; L&B recording artist and blues singer; Charles Street Foundation board member.

Robin's Diary

January 23, 1994

I'm going to write this down so I can rid my brain of it and get on to the important elements in my life, i.e., advanced logarithms, transcribing my notes on the metaphysical poets, and figuring out a wedding gift for Uncle Mac and Felicia. Oh, and the greatest excitement of the evening: ten new French verbs, two irregular. Big whoop.

The problem is I seem to have Michael Cates on the brain again, and it's not only distracting, it is starting to embarrass me, even in front of myself. The question is, why? Okay, he is not unattractive (okay, he is <u>very</u> attractive), but he is somewhat rude , fairly arrogant, anything but intellectual (a high school drop-out?!) with a questionable past, not to mention present, probably no morals or values. . . . Right. Like mine are so fine. Sure I've got them, but have they ever been tested? How do I know they aren't just <u>language</u>?

Anyway, how do you relate to someone who prefers to be called "Stone" when his name is really Michael? This alone should be a clue we don't inhabit the same wavelength. (Then why did it feel like we do?) It's so obviously a part of his tough-guy, street-kid, macho-cool image. And I told him so.

Maybe this is why he hasn't called.

So, who am I to knock it? I have an image to uphold myself: Robin Devane Scorpio, Thoroughly Excellent. Brilliant student, all-around awfully good girl, dutiful niece, truthful, brave, faithful, and boring. Not ugly but nothing great. I've been told different, but I know what I see. Five feet one inch tall; A-cup that doesn't promise much more. Long dark hair like my mother's. Eyes like hers, too, but without the flash. At least so far.

I have been told I have my father's smile, which wasn't exactly a smile but was about half a grin, with something under it that looked like a secret. Uncle Mac has it, too. I guess it's a Scorpio thing. Unfortunately, I have the look, but not the secret.

At least not yet. Maybe it will be "revealed to me," but somehow I doubt it, at least the way things are going.

Why am I wasting my time when I have a French test tomorrow babbling on paper about my personal appearance, insecurities, and other trivial issues? Get real, Robin—the only issue on your mind is Michael Cates. Michael "Stone" Cates, who keeps sauntering around in my head, with that put-on cynical cool look and those deep eyes that look right into you as though he knows you probably don't have any answers either.

Later, Verbs Digested

What's really bothering me is my ego, I suppose. After that day in Kelly's, when he specifically said, "Maybe we should do it again, on purpose. When you're not in such a hurry."

He meant have a conversation. My stomach flip-flopped. I guess I expected a call or something. Now I realize he didn't mean it. Stupid me.

Oh, well, we probably wouldn't have enough material for a next conversation. He said he liked my directness. Ha. Candor may be a fine quality, but it spells death to any male-female relationship. See? It already did.

January 25, 1994

Okay, so I'm obsessed; sue me. (Only Robin Scorpio would bother to punctuate that with a semi-colon.) There, see! Right there is the problem:

I'm sure Michael Cates, if he ever met a semi-colon, would put it in its proper place, which is nowhere in his life. (So how can I imagine that a person who thinks this much about punctuation could possibly have a place in his life, either?)

Probably this obsession has to do with my current boyfriendless state. The only boyfriend I've had so far was Roger Hollander, and I don't think we really liked each other. Then I had this large crush on Jason Quartermaine, who was very kind about it.

Maybe that's all this is about Mike Cates (okay, I'll give him <u>Mike</u>, but not <u>Stone</u>)—a raving crush. It feels like more, but how would I know? I may be some kind of sexual retard.

Tiffany keeps warning me about "raging hormones." I have reason to believe my hormones are awake, but they're not anywhere near raging. Felicia keeps assuring me I am probably a late bloomer. Then there's Brenda, who I guess bloomed early and could probably give me some advice, but I don't even know what to ask. Anyway, it's not any of their business.

Lucky for me, virginity has made a comeback. Given today's public health problems, abstinence is becoming cool. Still, I'd prefer it to be by choice.

Actually, I suspect the reason I don't have a boyfriend may have less to do with sexuality than with the conventions of communication, which I haven't exactly mastered. My never learning what you say and what you don't, or how to cover up what I really think until it's safe. And maybe I'm attracted to Mike Cates because he mostly can't be bothered. I guess living on the street doesn't equip you much in the way of niceties.

It's not that I don't know how to be polite. It's the space between "manners" and genuine connection that gives me trouble. Maybe I'm missing a gene.

And maybe Michael Cates is, too. Which is why he wouldn't give up his seat for me the night I met him. September, the match between A.J. and Jagger. (I loathe boxing as an institution, but this fight was almost a class struggle.)

Mike was sitting next to Brenda on the aisle. I came in late and she introduced us. I knew who he was, of course—Jagger's lost-and-found brother—but I'd never seen him. We said hello, I asked him to scoot down so I could take the aisle seat, and he directed me to the empty seat on the other side of Brenda! I said I liked the aisle, and he said so did he—and he got there first. "What a gentleman," I said, meaning what a creep.

He's been on my mind ever since.

February 3, 1994

I am going to murder Brenda Barrett! I am going to chop her gorgeous body into small manageable pieces and flush them. Turns out the reason Mike never followed up on seeing me again was that my friend Brenda had warned him off!!!

When I confronted her with this she wouldn't even apologize! Only for embarrassing me, but not for "trying to watch out" for me. Like I asked.

Like I need this. Then she says Mike is "bad news." She is the person who pointed out his assets to me in the first place! (Not that I hadn't noticed.)

I found all this out in the most mortifying way possible, of course—from Mike himself. I ran into him at Kelly's, and he just happened to mention that the day we'd all been there together Brenda had told him to keep his hands off!

I blurted out (see, there I go), "Just forget her, Mike. Forget whatever she said!" Subtle, huh? God, I am so humiliated.

February 5, 1994
Yes! A Next Conversation

Jagger and Karen brought him to the wedding with them (Mac and Felicia's, which turned suddenly into Jenny and Paul's), and I guess he was wandering around the party not knowing anyone, because he seemed strangely glad to see me.

If in fact I have this major communication problem, why is it so easy with him? The only thing hard is not to look at his face too much, because I'm afraid what I'm thinking is written all over mine. But talking, that is so easy.

Mike has a way of getting to the center of things, assuming you know where it is, too, and going on from there. He knew exactly how I must feel about what had just happened (Mac hurt, every-thing turned around): the feeling you are not in charge of anything that happens in your life, and whoever is doesn't know what they are doing.

What does he do about it? He says he tries harder not to care. If he has nightmares, he gets up and roams around by himself in the night. (The thought of this makes me hurt for him.) Tells me I could call him then (in the night) if I need to. I doubt I'd do that, but I am blown away by the invitation.

February 17, 1994

I ran into Mike again today. (Okay, I've been spending more time at Kelly's; it's the only place I've ever run into him.) He said he hadn't been in touch since the wedding because he thought my family probably didn't need any complications.

I was so glad he felt the need to explain that I couldn't think of anything to say back. He didn't seem to notice, asked if Mac and Felicia had set a date for a "rematch," so to speak, but I told him Maxie's sick with some weird thing (Kowasacki Syndrome) and it'd been shelved till she's better. He said he hoped that would be soon.

That is absolutely all that happened. Why am I so insanely happy?

February 25, 1994

So he finally made a move,

AND NOW I AM GROUNDED.

GROUNDED?!

I think Uncle Mac must have studied parenting techniques on Friday night sitcoms. The ones with the adorable families who learn warm, so-cute-you-could-throw-up lessons about life and love in half an hour? Of course these shows are on Friday because no self-respecting kid over twelve would be home that night, and the sponsors think they can con millions of middle-aged people into believing they understand their children.

Did Uncle Mac think it was cute to ground me? He is not an intrinsically mean person. Okay, I did something that I suppose from an adult-person-in-charge's point of view looks bad. But why can't he see it in the context with the rest of my behavior—my entire life? Does this cancel out all the effort I've made for as long as I can remember to be responsible and make them proud of me? Maybe I got tired of making them proud. And who are "they" anyway? Mac and Felicia? My mother and father?

There is a point where if you work your butt off to do remark-able things year after year, nobody finds them remarkable anymore. They are expected—no, required. You are stuck on a treadmill of excellence, and suddenly you look up and see the world waving all the things you've missed at you. The world, of course, being Mike Cates.

Here, for posterity, are the facts of my heinous behavior: Last night, February 24: Felicia was upstairs putting Maxie to bed. Mac was at the Outback. I was in the middle of my usual ninety pounds of homework when the doorbell rang.

I went to answer and checked the peephole (a habit drilled into me since I had to get on a chair to do it) and almost stopped breathing, then felt like an idiot.

I opened the door and Michael Cates is standing there, so non-chalantly you'd think it was usual, and he smiles this outrageous smile he has and just says, "hey." Great opening. To which I respond brilliantly with, "hi," and then stand there like a dweeb staring at him.

He finally explains he was just hanging and saw our light, though what is strange about having a light on at nine o'clock in the evening I don't know. "Homework," I say stupidly. "Drag," he says, and asks if he gets to come in "or what." This makes me very tense, wondering what "or what" is, but I let him in.

He stares at my assembled homework stuff like it is material from another planet, and we get into an immediate discussion about why good grades are or aren't worth the trouble.

He has this "why bother" attitude, which I suppose comes from years of being tossed around and nobody caring. It's not that he's dumb—you can tell he's smart by the way he argues—but he questions a whole lot of things I take for granted, like "the work ethic."

We are in the middle of this philosophical debate, and I am trying unsuccessfully to be unaware of his eyes, and he is, I'm afraid, aware of my effort, when Uncle Mac walks in and immediately goes all suspicious. I am totally mortified. (It is interesting how much time I've spent in that condition since I've known Mike Cates.)

I introduce them, which is hardly necessary, since Uncle Mac spent so much time looking for him for Jagger last year, and when I look at Michael I see that a humongous chip has been hefted onto his gorgeous shoulder. There is a somewhat negative exchange in which Mike blows off the idea of school and Uncle Mac blows off the idea of him, and all but tosses him out of the house!

I can barely talk, I am so furious and humiliated, and when I gasp out, "That's the most horrible thing you've ever done to me," Uncle Mac makes this huge pronouncement: "He is not for you." Like that. Zeus or somebody has spoken. Then I get the "I am responsible for you" lecture I've gotten every time in the last two and a half years that I've wanted to do something he didn't want me to do (and always wound up not doing it).

I point out he doesn't even know Mike, but he is on Automatic, now into "I-care-what-happens-to-you-Robin" mode. Though obviously he doesn't care what I think or feel. He wants to "air this out" now, but I know this just means more pronouncements, so I leave and go to my room with my books.

Five minutes later there is a little sound on my window—a little haphazard tapping sound. I think it is a squirrel or a branch or something, but it keeps up, and I go and look out and it is Mike. He has climbed up onto the extension roof. I am still hideously embarrassed, and I apologize for Mac's rotten treatment of him, but he only seems to think it's funny and asks if I have plans for the rest of the evening. I do not consider the question long.

I grab my coat and climb out the window onto the roof and over to the terrace. Mike is impressed by my agility, says I must've been doing this for years. No, I say, I've been <u>waiting</u> for years.

And I go off with him feeling freer and bolder than I have in my whole life.

The upshot is because I am overly enthusiastic in the pool hall—I believe my words were, "I'm ready to kick some butt"—we get noticed and not just carded, but the manager takes one look at me and calls home. The rest is history. I apologize to Uncle Mac, but he isn't having any. I point out that his behavior was less than brilliant, too, but he doesn't take it well. I go upstairs and think about the feeling of Mike's arms around me, teaching me how to hold a cue.

Coaster from Jake's Billiards. Maybe I'll celebrate my 18th birthday there.

JAKE'S **8** BILLIARDS

Keep your eye on the ball

March 3, 1994

Oh, what beautiful irony! Due to Uncle Mac's brilliant detective work, which ended in more or less reuniting the Cates family, Mike and I are going to wind up in the same wedding party, and there is nothing Mac can do about it!

Maybe when he sees that Mike is perfectly able to function under these circumstances (wearing a tux, making a toast, etc.), he will change his tune. Providing Mike is able to function. Or I should say chooses to, given his opinions on the formalities of society. I don't think Mike would do anything that would hurt Jagger, though, so he'll probably make an effort.

Anyway, when Mike found out I was going to be Karen's maid of honor, he said maybe the wedding would be "some fun, after all." But maybe I'm reading too much in.

On the other hand, when I contemplate Michael Cates in a tuxedo, I get so stupidly weak I can't believe it. (The only thing I would like to see more is Michael Cates without a shirt on, and the thought of that makes me even weaker.)

March 5, 1994

I am worried about Brenda and I am worried about Mike. I see the following equations:

$$\textit{Brenda Barrett + Sonny Corinthos = Trouble}$$
$$\textit{Mike Cates + Sonny Corinthos = Trouble}$$

Of course, Uncle Mac would add:

$$\textit{Robin Scorpio + Mike Cates = Trouble}$$

But that is an equation that can't be proved. In fact, it is the opposite of the truth. I may be able to keep Mike out of trouble, just by being a good influence. But Brenda, I don't know.

Uncle Mac let me off the leash briefly, and I went to Kelly's, where I watched her cozying up to Sonny. This both repelled and fascinated me. She can't seem to help herself. Granted he is a very sexy guy, if you like that type. He has that broody, sulky, smoldering quality some women find irresistible. Now Mike has a certain broodiness about him, but it is much more—I don't know—innocent? Well maybe not innocent, exactly, but vulnerable. And there is a sweetness . . . oh, for God's sake. I am embarrassing myself again.

The point is (was supposed to be), I'm scared because Sonny Corinthos is dangerous. Ask Karen. Not just because he ran a strip joint where she worked underage (which has since been closed down by the cops), but because he has what Ruby calls "dubious connections." I hate the implication, because Mike works for him. When I ask him what he does for Sonny he says, "this and that," which makes me even more nervous. He also says things are getting "big time." I hope he is just swaggering.

I wish Brenda would stay away from Sonny. He is all wrong for her. Maybe it's the element of danger that attracts her. Actually, I understand this way too well, because of my mother and Duke. Okay, it wasn't until after he was my stepfather that she found out about his line of work, but he had that same dark fascination from the start. Even for me. Wonderful mystery in his face, but love and decency there, too.

I just got a chill; I realized that also applies to Michael Cates. But I can't believe there's any danger in Mike. Maybe some arrogance and some devil-may-care stuff that could get him in trouble, but I know—I can tell—he's intrinsically a gentle person and would never really hurt anyone. Especially me. Because (can I say it at least here?) I think he likes me quite a lot.

I wish he'd stay away from Sonny, too. But that's very unlikely. Sonny's the one who picked him up off the street and cleaned him up and gave him a job and a break—and the name "Stone," which I hate—and Mike is thoroughly loyal and grateful. These are admirable qualities, right, Uncle Mac????

The thing is, even in the brief time I've known Mike I've gotten able to read him pretty well. There is a kind of shorthand between us; I don't know why, it's just there. Even though we disagree on a lot of basic things, there is a quick gut understanding. I feel it coming from him, too.

And what I sense under his excitement and tension about Sonny and his business is a kind of "cops and robbers" feeling, which makes me remember when I was little and played with the kids next door: it was always more fun to be the bad guys.

March 30, 1994
Karen and Jagger's Wedding

Incredibly moving and beautiful. Why do we cry when we're happy? Why does the sight of Karen in the gown her mother made her, moving slowly toward Jagger in the candlelight at Kelly's of all places (but how right, how right for them!) make us spill over with tears? Is it because we know what they went through to get there? I suppose it's partly that, but I think it's bigger. It is something important that is continuing—<u>hope</u>, I guess, that two people can really touch each other in a way that changes them both and

K & J's
Big day!

Ribbon and flower
from my bouquet.
My dress was
wine-colored velvet.
Mike said I looked
cool in it.

makes the whole equal to more than "the sum of its parts," and in the process maybe even benefits the world.

Is that adolescently idealistic? Probably, considering the divorce rate, but that's what I mean—it's not the actuality, it's the brave attempt. I wonder if I'll ever have the nerve.

I saw tears in Mike's eyes, too, though I'm sure he would deny it. That's such a sad thing about men, that they aren't allowed tears. Maybe there's been some breakthrough in attitude, but not much. It's probably why women live longer.

I bet unshed tears can clog up your veins like cholesterol, so that everything going to and from your heart gets impacted. Maybe that's what's wrong with Uncle Mac.

April 10, 1994

Maybe I should stop fighting it and call him Stone. I didn't realize I was being controlling and arrogant. Not that he said so. He implied and I inferred. I kept addressing him as Mike at the wedding. He's never called me on it. But I noticed Gina called him that, too, and I mentioned it, and he said oh sure she would, because it's part of her fantasy.

His sister, he says, thinks that he is still the same person he was, or was going to be, when he was eight and Jagger was twelve and she was six, before the family split. Before she was "adoped rich," as he puts it, and he and Jagger went out on their own and they all lost each other.

When Sonny found him and took him off the street he gave him the name Stone for "rolling stone," which is what he pretty much was then. For some reason Stone takes a certain pride in this—maybe the pride of simple survival. But if that's what he wants to be called, who am I to call him something else?

Okay, okay, I'll call him Stone. Actually I'm beginning to kind of like the sound of it.

April 14, 1994

This has been the most amazing day of my life. Michael Stone Cates kissed me, but it wasn't just <u>that</u> he kissed me, it was the <u>way</u> he kissed me, and the way I felt before, during, and afterward, and even now, because I can still feel it.

He showed up at the house this afternoon, at a bad time, of course, but when would be a good time as far as Uncle Mac's concerned? Still, it was particular chaos, because we had just gotten Maxie home from the hospital and things were tense, and Kevin Collins had shown up, which put Uncle Mac in a worse mood, and then to have Stone walk in on top of that was entirely too much.

Uncle Mac was less than gracious, but I guess that didn't bother Stone. Maybe he considers it a challenge, or it just amuses him to watch Uncle Mac go off, but I got him out of there pretty fast and we went for a walk in the park.

There is nothing like the smell of April: damp earth and new flowers and everything starting over. The whole sense of possibility.

I was trying to explain the family dynamic to Stone, and he asked a question that threw me: was that the way I spent all my time—figuring out everybody else's trip, and had I given any thought to mine? (Take note, Uncle Mac, this is not a loser asking these questions; this is a person with insight.)

I admitted my m.o., at least for the past few years, has pretty much been keeping quiet and not adding to anyone's problems. He wondered what was in this for me. I'd never thought about it. I said, only about half-kidding, "Virtue is its own reward." He seemed unconvinced.

We were quiet for a while, just sitting there on a bench. I closed my eyes and could feel the sun on my face and the sense of him next to me and this strange peaceful feeling of simply <u>being</u>, without effort. I could feel him looking at me, and when I opened my eyes I was staring straight into his. He said, and I'll never forget the sound of it: "You are so pretty . . . so sweet." And he took me in his arms and kissed me, slowly and gently and thoroughly. It was total bliss.

April 15, 1994

I woke up thinking about it, and replaying it the way you play the track of a song you love, over and over. If I remember hard enough I can get some of it back—the actual feeling of his arms coming around me and the split-second sense of omigosh it's happening, and as it did, the small jolt in the bottom of my stomach that resembles the feeling you get when you plunge down the first hill of a roller coaster—only it is a smaller, much more intimate jolt—nothing to scream about or be scared about. It's to go with.

Not that I had a choice. Something just took over: my heart raced (cliché, but there it was) and I felt kind of weak and weird. (Good weird. Very good.)

Amazing that your body has a memory of its own. Sense memory, I guess. I wonder, scientifically, what is happening—cells remembering the pressure of cells? Neurons sailing over a synapse and saying that was nice, could we try it again?

Stone said, after he kissed me (after we'd been quiet awhile, my head on his shoulder, his head resting on mine) that he wanted to see me again. I want that too (so much!), but I know how miserable Uncle Mac will be about it.

I would like to go to Felicia, because I suspect she thinks Mac's being unreasonable, but I also know she'd never dispute his authority. Besides, she's got enough on her mind with Maxie.

Who I'd really like to talk to is Karen, but she is off being a newlywed and you're not supposed to bother them. Maybe I'll try Brenda. She's really turned out to be a better friend than I would have expected, though God knows her judgment is a bit flawed.

Same, 3 P.M.

Now I'm really nervous, because Brenda got this wild idea, and when Brenda gets a wild idea she usually does it. I'd been worried about discussing the kiss, because she'd warned me off Stone, but she said as long as he truly appreciates me, she's cool with it. Maybe she's rationalizing her own thing with Sonny, but I'm grateful for anything positive at this point.

Anyway, she had this date to have dinner with Sonny, in his apartment. Alone. So she suggested I tell Mac that I was having dinner with her. I balked at this, not because I'm so moral, but I've never learned to lie decently. I know how to keep my mouth shut about some things, but to out and out lie, I don't know, I get all strange. Especially with Uncle Mac. However, Brenda pointed out it wouldn't be a lie: I <u>would</u> have dinner with her. We just wouldn't mention the rest of it.

Brenda is really good at getting around things. Like, when Mac asked straight out if there would be boys there, she looked at him dead on and said, "How can we talk about boys if there are boys there?" Maybe this is why she is the Deception Girl.

Then she called Sonny and set it up as a "double date." How fifties. I'm sure Sonny's thrilled. All I know is my stomach's already doing cartwheels.

It's not so much that I'm going where I probably shouldn't go, with people the Management doesn't want me to see. It's that I'm afraid I'll say something stupid and unsophisticated that will make everyone laugh and I won't know why. Or that Stone will be bored to death and wonder why he ever kissed me in the first place.

April 16, 1994

Straight downhill to disaster from there. My Grandma Filomena used to say life has the peaks and the valleys, but I sure would have liked to stay on that peak a little longer. So I tried, and now I'm in more trouble than I've ever been in in my life.

Stone wanted to take the blame, figuring Mac hates him anyway, but I couldn't let him. I have to Take Responsibility for my own actions: I drank the wine, I was driving illegally, I floored the thing. Maybe some of it was Stone's idea, but I could have said no.

Going up the stairs at Sonny's, I almost ran down again. But when we got inside I could see that Stone was a little nervous, too, so I relaxed some, if that makes any sense.

And here is something that will straighten Uncle Mac's hair: I can't help it, I kind of like Sonny Corinthos. He was what they call a "gracious host," offering hors d'oeuvres, pouring wine (except for me, but he didn't make an issue of it), and generally putting people at ease. (I poured my own glass later on and he didn't make an issue of that, either. Maybe he didn't notice.)

Sonny is very polite and quite funny. I like it that he is able to laugh at himself. What I really like is the way he is with Stone—sort of familial. Stone needs that so much.

17

So I can see why Brenda was drawn to him (besides the obvious), and it's hard to reconcile all the rumors and the fact that he almost ruined Karen's life.

I know this much: nobody is all black and white. Everybody has gray areas, and it is quite possible to like a person without trusting him.

Sonny trusts Stone, though, enough to give him the keys to the Jaguar (like I'm dumb enough not to realize he wanted to be alone with Brenda?). And Stone trusted me enough to let me drive.

It felt fabulous, gunning twelve cylinders, riding that power. Made me think of what Brenda said to Karen: "Grab onto it, ride it like the wind, and know you have every right to it." She was talking about happiness. I remember her words because they were so unusual for her. Brenda is not a poetic type.

So I grabbed and rode, right up to 82 miles an hour for maybe two whole minutes, Stone laughing beside me, until the flashing red gumballs appeared behind us.

I almost freaked at the police station, but Stone was very cool and calm, probably trying to show me how to act. I guess he'd been fingerprinted before.

There will be a hearing some time in the future when the Law decides what to do with me. God forbid anyone should give me a break. Uncle Sean tried, but Uncle Mac wouldn't let him. In the meantime I am grounded forever. (Six weeks.)

I know I made a big mistake, but I've gained Wisdom and Humility from it. (Plus being scared out of my skull and losing my permit.) Couldn't that be enough?

Does one dumb mistake have to have such stupid, heavy consequences?

April 30, 1994

The last two weeks have been so awful around here. I feel like I have some kind of Dread Disease or something. Felicia isn't mean, but she's distant—partly distracted about Maxie and partly being careful about Uncle Mac's sacred Authority. He and I do everything we can to avoid each other.

Then today things got worse with Maxie and they had to take

her to the hospital again. I am so, so scared for her, and I can't do anything. Not anything.

Please. Maxie is my little sister. It doesn't matter that the wedding hasn't happened yet—she is. I've never had a sibling and it's one of the best things about Mac and Felicia getting together. I am going to teach her to dive this summer. I already promised, and it has to happen. Too many promises have been broken. That isn't good for a child.

This morning I waited in my room, like I've been doing every day, till I knew Uncle Mac was gone, scarfed down one of Felicia's health food breakfast bars (sawdust paste between two layers of cardboard) and started to leave for school, and I just couldn't do it.

Things are so unreal there. I wonder why I never—no matter what I do—feel connected. I get my A's, I mind my business, I have conversations with my classmates, but I think about 10 percent of me is engaged. The rest of me is miserable and scared and angry and most of all lonely. The only person I want to see is Stone.

Later

He was here in ten minutes. I honestly didn't mean to lay all my misery on him, but he seemed to know that I needed to sound off. It felt so incredibly good to be heard. I realized then that he's more than a romantic interest; he's a really good friend. I wonder if that's unusual. (To have both, in one package.)

Mac or no Mac, no way am I going to stop seeing Stone. I need him too much. What I do not need is my uncle walking in on us and blowing a gasket, ranting and raving about his precious rules! If he's afraid for me, why can't he understand that Stone is saving my life by just listening? Why do I have to defend everything wonderful?

I feel like I'm yelling at the top of my voice. Why can't Mac hear me? I want to tell him I still need him, but not for telling me how to think or what to do. I need his support, and I'd like his approval. But I can and I will live without it if I have to.

Still, he is the only true "family" I have. I like my uncle. I admire him, and I love him. His going after Frisco, to bring him back for Maxie, was the most generous, heroic thing I ever heard of. And if anyone had tried to stop him or warned him that he could get hurt, he'd have done it anyway, right? Because it was what he needed to do.

Not that I don't sympathize: it has to be hard, inheriting a 14-year-old girl from your brother. (Let me tell you, it's not so easy being inherited, either.) But I'm not 14 anymore, and "guardian" doesn't mean you establish a 24-hour watch over a person.

He says he has good instincts and they scream at him that Stone is wrong for me. Dammit, Uncle Mac, your instincts don't apply to my life!

May 30, 1994

So much, so awful in a month. So many changes. Maxie nearly died. B.J. <u>did</u> die. And because she did, Maxie didn't.

Mac and Felicia are not getting married—Mac's decision. Which means the family we had constructed—Mac, Felicia, Maxie, and I—will not continue to exist as such after all. I suppose you could say that died, too.

He assures me this doesn't have to change my relationship with Felicia, but that is typical of Uncle Mac: it won't happen because he says so. Wrong again, Mac. Of course Felicia and I will be friends, but for a while there it was almost like having a mother again.

I don't understand things like what happened to B.J. There's been a lot of death in my life—some of it I've seen firsthand. Memories so horrific there is no feeling to them at all—they are too dangerous: Grandma Fil. Duke. Duke was too young to die, and so were my mother and father. But B.J. was a child. Six. Someone drives drunk (drives <u>drunk</u>, Robin) and hits a school van. Maxie, dying in the hospital, waits for a heart and gets her cousin's. It seems totally bizarre and totally arbitrary. What is God thinking of? Is there a God who thinks at all?

These are questions I ask Stone, and he doesn't pretend to know, but he just holds me and I feel less alone. He says no matter what happens I'll be okay, because I am a survivor and so is he—that it's one of the things we have in common.

I never thought about it, but I suppose it's true. He'd been shocked to find out that I had a fairly harrowing childhood. Probably thought I was the soul of normalcy. He should only know how hard I've worked to make it look that way.

"Normal" doesn't seem so important anymore. I was probably going after it because I knew that's what my parents wanted more than anything for me: a truly "normal" life. (Interesting that Stone lost his family at about the same age I found mine.)

But now what they wanted is less important than what I want. I don't think that's selfish; I think growing up is about figuring out what that is. Right now what I want is Stone Cates. More and more of him.

June 8, 1994

I may as well buy myself a T-shirt that says:

GO AHEAD,
INTERFERE WITH MY LIFE AND WHILE YOU'RE AT IT,
TOTALLY EMBARRASS ME

I hadn't seen Stone or talked to him since right after Maxie's operation. We'd all been spending so much time at the hospital, and I didn't want to rock the boat with Uncle Mac, especially when he was hurting over cancelling the wedding. He never told me exactly why, so I guess I will never know, because I won't ask. I try to <u>respect people's privacy</u>.

Anyway, I'd been missing Stone so much I finally had to call him, which is a good thing, because he'd actually begun to wonder if I'd given in to Uncle Mac's edict, but I said no, it was just the chaos here. He seemed to understand, but I <u>think</u> he was relieved. (I hope.)

It was so good to have his arms around me again and just talk, and when we weren't talking, kiss a lot. You would think, wouldn't you, that after you'd kissed a person that much it would get old?

Maybe it will, but not so far. Anyway, that's what we were doing when Felicia came in. That's all we were doing, and all that we intended to do. She was pretty cool, and we were pretty matter-of-fact about it, though Stone left fairly soon after that.

Next thing I know Felicia is sitting me down for what she bills as a "frank discussion about sex." I want to run screaming from the room—I try—but she starts in with how we are still family, whether she's married to Mac or not, and how families Share. I wanted to say I was an only child and I never learned to Share, but she had obviously warmed to the role.

It's not like we've never discussed the subject before, but we were talking principles then, not possibilities. What was making me squirm was that this was personal, involving My (alleged) sex life. Oh, and just to relax me, she starts talking about her and Uncle Mac and how long they waited, and I prayed for the floorboards to open up and swallow me before she got specific.

They didn't, and she didn't, but I managed a weak protest and she said she was only leading into her point that the best solution to sex in the 90s was not to have any until you get married. And you shouldn't get married unless you've both been tested for HIV. Like this is new information.

Like I must be going to have sex just because Stone is kissing me in the living room! I explained to her I wasn't having sex and I wasn't planning to, but she came right back with "You can't always plan it." Get this: "Passion is an overwhelming emotion." Well, duh. I just wanted her to shut up, but she was relentless about how sometimes feelings get out of control and that the fear of pregnancy was one thing, but having sex with the wrong person nowadays could be a death sentence.

I swore to her I knew that. How can you not know about Safe Sex with school programs and TV and books and magazines bombarding you with the information? But, I kept telling her, it is entirely hypothetical because

I am not having Sex
and I will not be Having Sex
Any Time Soon.

(Maybe I should get that on a T-shirt.)

She said she understood my discomfort, but it just proved that we had to get these things out in the open and . . . oh, God, this really happened . . . "just to be sure, even with the best intentions, it is best to be prepared" . . . and she reaches in her purse and brings out this condom, which she presents to me with the question, "Do you know how to use it?"

I wanted to say, "Gee, I must be really dumb, I thought the guy was the one who used it," but I was too afraid she was going to bring out a cucumber and demonstrate, so I dropped the condom and ran. I guess she figured she'd made her point, because at least she didn't run after me waving the thing.

That ought to have been horrible enough for one day, right? Not, because shortly after that Uncle Mac comes in to have a "discussion" about my summer plans. Or I should say, his summer plans, which are for me to work at the Outback to earn the money for the humongous fine they're going to slap on me at my hearing. I object, but only weakly, and then give in because I have a more important objective—which is to get him to soften up about Stone. I argue he doesn't know Stone at all and he has the audacity to say he does, because Stone reminds him of himself twenty years ago when he was up to no good!

I can't believe he's inflicting his guilt on my relationship. I am ready to yell "Carry your own baggage!" when we are diverted in a terrible way. Mac looks down at an object he picked up from the coffee table and has been fiddling with to keep his hands busy. (God, why did he have to stop smoking?) What he sees is Felicia's condom.

So I am forced for the second time in a day (isn't this some kind of child abuse?) to undergo a lecture on a subject I consider intensely personal by a person whom I respect but do not want to discuss it with! He asks point blank (promising he will not yell) if I'm sexually active. I swear I'm not, I swear I'm not planning to be any time soon. (Maybe never. I'm beginning to think a convent looks good if it will stop all this revolting frankness.)

And get this—which would be hilarious if it didn't make me so crazy—he wants me to feel free to turn to him if I ever want to talk about it. I yell "Never!" and finally get to run screaming from the room.

June 9, 1994

Inevitably, since it's all anyone seems to want to talk about here, I have been thinking about sex. In the first place, what is the meaning of the phrase "having sex?" It is, to say the least, grammatically incorrect. Sex is not something that you have, except as it is inherent in one's physical (and, arguably, mental and emotional makeup.) And sex is not something that you <u>do</u>, despite the popularity of the construction "doing it." I guess the antecedent to "it" there is the act of sexual intercourse. Now there's a phrase that's a real turn-on.

Then there's "sexual congress" (which invokes all kinds of funny mental pictures). And according to the thesaurus, there's "coitus" and "copulation," both of which have always made me think of farm animals. And of course there are any number of vulgar terms which I won't sully these virginal pages with. (I know I just ended a sentence with a preposition, but let's try to stay with the program here.) Oh, yes, and there's the old stand-by, "making love." Whatever that may mean.

My English teacher, Ms. Harper, bemoans the graphic portrayal of sex in today's literature, particularly movies and television (which she is broad-minded enough to include in the term) and the fact that we have robbed our young people of what she calls their "right to mystery."

I guess I know what she means because it's true—there isn't much one hasn't seen laid out (you'll excuse the expression) on the screen in considerable detail. Now this woman must be 50, but apparently still has hormones, because she read a poem of John Donne's in class ("Elegy XIX, To His Mistress Going to Bed") in such a way that it invoked the most sexual feeling I'd ever had (until April 14).

It's not so much what I'm getting at as what I'm avoiding here. No, Felicia, no, Mac, I am not having, nor do I plan in the near future to have sex. But have I thought about it? Have I thought about it, specifically, with Stone Cates?

. . . What's the point of having a diary if you tell lies in it? God, <u>yes</u>. I've thought about it a lot.

June 10, 1994

From the time Stone first kissed me I have felt like something major is happening in that direction. Like I must have been asleep from the neck down and that woke me up.

When I think about Stone it's not just with my head. All of me is involved. I guess this is normal. I'm sure it was to be expected. I just didn't expect it to be quite like this.

(Memo to Tiffany: The hormones aren't exactly raging yet, but they are going a little berserk.) <u>Nevertheless</u>, I am carefully monitoring this, and it is under control. Stone (yes, Uncle Mac, Stone) is being a gentleman. The kisses are hot, but that's it. For now. There is too much to know about each other. And how do you separate simple lust (me????) from the rest of the relationship?

I want to crawl back into my head where it is safe. It is getting warm here.

June 12, 1994

Stone Cates Stone Cates Stone Cates

I can't believe I just did that. ⬆ How adolescent can you get? Okay, I know technically I <u>am</u> an adolescent, but I have always been so sensible and mature. I am now reduced to liquid by a phone call.

June 13, 1994

I have decided to deal with this in an organized, intelligent, scholarly way. I will confront the question—Responsibly—so as not, some time in the fairly distant future, to be "swept away," (Felicia's term) with <u>passion</u>. (For some reason, that's a word that makes me blush—not the concept, it's just so trash-novel sounding.)

That is, in order to avoid yielding to the above mindlessly, I thought I would give some thought to and get straight in advance my personal . . .

<u>Criteria for Making Love</u>*
*Of all the lame referents examined in my earlier entry on this subject, this seems the least offensive, and closest to what I would-hope it would be.

Requirements.

1. Love

   (A) Both be in

   (B) Clarity on what is

25

2. Commitment

      (A) To what?

      (B) Long-term??

3. Want to

      (A) Both must, as opposed to:

      (B) Pleasing the other party

4. Meaningful, i.e.,

      (A) Important; significant; momentous

      (B) Not just a fling or answering a physical need

5. About US (whoever that may be), not anyone else, as in

      (A) Rebellion against Authority (who shall remain nameless)

      (B) Jealousy of third party, threatened by same

6. Unsordid, untacky

      (A) Reasonably romantic and decent physical situation (as opposed to drive-in movie cheap motel, etc.)

7. Safe

      (A) Protected against pregnancy

      (B) Protected against sexually transmitted disease

"Well-considered, Robin . . ." (Ms. Harper's favorite comment). A-plus for forethought (as opposed to foreplay, I guess. Haha).

Of course, it might just squelch spontaneity, but you can't have everything. So what should I do with the list? Pin it to my bra? Keep it in an envelope in my purse, with Felicia's gift-condom? (Can't, of course, since Mac confiscated that.) Engrave it on my psyche? Recite it aloud when things are in danger of Going Too Far? I don't know, but it gives me satisfaction to have thought it through. (All the satisfaction I'm likely to get for a while, I guess.)

June 14, 1994

Uncle Mac is driving me crazy, all cheerful and acting like nothing was ever wrong between us and won't we have barrels of fun with me slaving at the Outback all summer. As far as I'm concerned one long hot boring back-breaking lonely summer is what I'm in for.

SO I have hatched a fantastic plan that can't fail to win Mac's approval for Stone. All I have to do is talk Stone into it. My plan is at once bold and brilliant. (This is no time to be modest. It will require a lot of confidence, and since Stone probably won't have any about this, I'll have to have it for both of us.)

The burning question is, will Michael Rolling-Stone-Off-the-Street Cates agree to do a scene from ROMEO AND JULIET with me for the Nurses' Ball? It should be an interesting test of how much he Cares.

I must be out of my mind. I'm setting myself up. Never mind how innately sensitive he is. Do I actually expect a former juvie to wear tights and spout Shakespeare in front of 500 people just to impress my uncle?

Maybe.

Later

If I ever wondered how much Stone likes me I now know, because he said yes. When I first asked him, he was appalled (more about the tights than the prospect of acting, I think), but when I told him the object was to raise his stock with Mac, he got into it. Also, and this is amazing to me, he'd never read anything by Shakespeare.

Why this surprises me, I don't know. Did I think they held seminars on the street? I don't know what I thought, but this one fact brought home more than anything he's ever told me how alone he was, and how disconnected from life as I know it. I mean, I've done my share of hiding, but someone else was always in charge, always taking care of me. The thought of how it must have been for him makes me want to take care of him forever.

But he's willing. Willing to try to bridge the difference and do it publicly. And Uncle Mac doesn't think he's motivated???

June 15, 1994

How can it be so much fun working on a death scene? (I believe this is known as paradox.) Stone had a lot of trouble reading the scene and even more comprehending it, I guess because so many of the words were unfamiliar, but he picked up on the acting part right away. I think he really has talent!

I could see he was struggling to learn the lines, so I suggested getting a tape from the library. He didn't even know there were such things as recorded plays. Obviously he doesn't have a library card, so I'll pick up a tape for him tomorrow after school.

June 17, 1994

I still don't believe it. I gave him the tape last night, and today when we met to rehearse he knew the whole scene by heart. He says he learns better when he hears something than when he reads it.

You can tell he responds to the rhythm of the poetry just by the way he says the lines, even when he doesn't quite understand them. He's really good! (Who knew? All I wanted was a display of devotion. Wouldn't it be funny if I'd launched him on a stage career?!) I think he likes the fact that we get to kiss in public. So do I. Uncle Mac, eat your heart out.

Still, I have enough faith in Mac to know he'll have to recognize the kind of effort and courage it will take Stone to do this. If he doesn't, at least he won't be able to throw a fit in front of most of Port Charles society. And he can't very well complain we've been seeing each other, when it's to benefit a good cause (The General Hospital AIDS programs).

I am going to add to my wardrobe of T-shirts:

Well-Intentioned But Doomed
To Humiliating Failure

Did I say Uncle Mac wouldn't be able to throw a fit in public? Wrong. Well, semi-public, backstage at the ball. Accusing me of disobeying <u>Orders</u>! <u>Orders</u>?! Where do you get off, Mac? Did you have to ruin something wonderful for us? Well, you didn't. I won't let you. It's a great memory, and you're not going to take it away, no matter how much noise and embarrassment you inflict on everyone.

Stone and I have come offstage, major applause, lots of hugs and congratulations, when Uncle Mac storms up and makes a total fool of himself and me. Then he storms on stage and does his "comedy" routine, which consists of a bunch of bad psychiatrist and teenager jokes (because he is also mad at Kevin, who had the nerve to congratulate Stone on his performance).

The weird thing is, the audience loved it. They thought he was hilarious. (Of course half of them were probably sloshed.) You'd think public approval might have mellowed him a little, but he came offstage in the same snit. Stone and I were still in the wings trying to get back the good feeling we had, when I hear this gasp out on the floor. I peek out of the curtains and there is Kevin Collins, Eminent Psychiatrist, standing with cream pie dripping off his face. It seems my uncle, the Adult who is Responsible for me and from whom I am supposed to take Orders, has thrown it at him!

This is maturity? So now what do I do? My plan totally backfired. Uncle Mac is madder than ever at Stone and felt I was taking a shot at him casting us as Romeo and Juliet in front of everybody. I wonder if this is guilt talking. If it is, he isn't listening, because we just went 'round and 'round with the same old pro-Stone, anti-Stone arguments, and got absolutely nowhere.

Well, I don't plan to listen, either. Not to him, anyway.

Back to my Romeo: he was amazing and beautiful. We were so in tune you'd think we'd known each other back in that century. Maybe we did. I hope we had an easier time of it than R & J, or than we're having now.

*I had to sit at Mac's table.
Stone had to sit at Sonny's.
Maybe next year . . .*

General Hospital Nurses' Ball

Robin Scorpio
Table 4

General Hospital Nurses' Ball

Stone Cates
Table 17

June 29, 1994

Another shining day. I stood before a court of law, some loving, caring friends (my legal guardian was there, too), and experienced the Consequences of my Behavior last April: $350, a rehab class for convicted drunk drivers, and my right to obtain a driver's license is revoked until I'm <u>eighteen</u>!

That do it for you, Uncle Mac? He swears he took no satisfaction in it, but he looked like he'd just eaten Thanksgiving dinner. I hope he gets gas.

Then he has the nerve to expect me to come to work at the Outback. That's when I blew up, right in his face, right there in the courthouse, in front of Felicia and Kevin and Stone and assorted strangers. I don't know what happened, but something hot surged from the bottom of my feet right up to my face and out of my mouth. And I said NO! To his face. And a number of other unpleasant things. After which I said I was going for a walk with Stone, and that's what I did. Uncle Mac looked almost as shocked as I was.

July 1, 1994

I've come up with the perfect counterattack: I'm going to grow nails like Lois Cerullo's. Just kidding. I couldn't bring it off. I've been hearing about her all this time from Brenda. Yards and yards. Maybe I'm even a little jealous? I used to be Brenda's best friend. Now it's Lois. Then again, Brenda used to be my best friend. Now it's Stone.

Lois is an experience. (An experience I'm glad I had today because her coming into the Outback averted another nasty fight with Mac.) I realized then I'd seen her before—Brenda had brought her to Karen and Jagger's wedding—but I never put it together that she was the "L" in L & B, the music company she and Brenda are trying to get off the ground. The one being financed by Sonny Corinthos . . .

How is it all roads seem to lead back to Sonny? It seems he and Lois are old friends from the neighborhood where they grew up in Brooklyn. (Lois, besides being drop-dead gorgeous, has a Brooklyn accent that is so intense it's almost poetry.) She says the secret to her nails is gelatin. My bet is it's nerve.

I admire women with nerve. Not that I don't have <u>any</u>. I must,

31

sharing the genes of Robert and Anna Scorpio (Mac, too, for that matter) and considering the kind of trouble I've gotten into in the past six months. But how do you make it work _for_ you? Stone says I have a choice—to get along with Mac or to fight with him.

I'm still humiliated that I lost it like that in front of Stone, but it didn't seem to bother him at all. One thing I hate to be is out of control. Especially in front of anybody. Stone says he loses it all the time himself: "Stuff comes out of my mouth, I don't know why or how."

But he also said if he had someone who cared about him as much as Mac cares about me . . . and left me to finish the sentence. Okay, okay, maybe it's for the wrong reasons (I care more what Stone thinks of me than I do Uncle Mac), but I will try to work things out and not use Stone to avoid him. That's your "no-good punk from the streets," Mac.

July 6, 1994

Oh, God. "Stuff comes out of my mouth, I don't know why or how." It just popped out, and I don't know when it happened. I mean I didn't decide, it was simply there, as if it had been there all along, and I finally noticed.

We were at Sonny's place—(strictly off limits, but so is being with Stone at all) Stone was being sweet, saying he worried about making complications in my life, and I said, without thinking, "Complications are easy if you go through them with someone you love." He looked startled and I realized what I'd said and realized it was true: I _love_ Stone Cates.

Then we both got awkward. Maybe he thought I was waiting for him to say he loves me. But I honestly wasn't. I was too busy discovering the truth of it, and why I'd said it, which was fairly obvious: I wanted him to know.

Now I'm wondering when that started. What am I looking for— the official date—time—instant that marked the progress of like-a-lot to love, and what, precisely, is the difference?

I'm not sure it's a linear thing.

More like something that expanded in me and at the same time got deeper. Impossible to explain. I am a smart person who grasps difficult philosophical, mathematical, and scientific concepts easily. Why does this elude me?

I guess I'm in good company—thousands of years of literary attempts to describe and explain the phenomenon. This is why we have metaphor. This is why we have poets. I'm no poet; right now I prefer to participate.

Last night was incredible. New. It's as though the person I really am, underneath Robin Perfection, and the person he really is, underneath Stone Tough and Cool, managed to reach each other and connect in some fundamental way.

I am not talking sex here, although those feelings were certainly there. It was more as if both of us had been lost, and maybe we're not exactly found now, but it'll be easier to look for a way out together.

And yes, there _was_ a different feeling when we kissed: more intense, closer, wanting more . . . and get this, Uncle Mac, it was Stone who pulled back. The truth is I didn't want him to. He was the one who said maybe we were moving too fast, and unfortunatey I had to agree. This is the person Mac thinks is a bad influence.

"...And she as much in love, her means much
                              less.
To meet her new beloved anywhere.
But passion lends them power, time means,
                              to meet,
Temp'ring extremities with extreme sweet."

R & J, Act II Prologue

33

July 7, 1994

Night of total madness, intrigue, and popcorn. I'm babysitting Maxie; Stone visits. With Felicia's permission? Well, no. Couldn't put her on the spot like that, but she wouldn't mind. I'm sure she thinks Mac's unreasonable. (She approved of Stone's Romeo, right?)

We settle on the couch, conversing and munching popcorn, idiotically trying to toss some in each other's mouth. (Sonny should see Stone in this mode.) Someone starts to throw handfuls. (Me.) Popcorn fight erupts, the two of us giggling and tickling, carrying on like crazed eight-year-olds.

Suddenly the sound of a car in the drive. Felicia's home early! Stone makes for the closet, but I redirect him to the window. He's out the window, fast! Fe and Tiff arrive to find me, dishevelled but innocent-looking, in a sea of popcorn.

My quick and agile story: watching horror movie, I was startled by their car, tossed the whole bowl. Stone is still hiding in bushes when Mac comes to pick me up.

Really, though, the fun was worth the scare. I never knew loving someone could be so entertaining.

Actual popcorn, retrieved when I undressed that night, from what would be my cleavage, if I had any.

July 22, 1994

Why can't we just be together in a simple way? I'd give anything for an old-fashioned date. The summer is gorgeous (what I can tell of it, from inside the Outback), one bright blue day after another. I want us to take a hike in the woods, have a picnic and an unthreatened conversation. How depraved of me.

Today Stone came by the Outback (checking first that Mac's car was gone) and lured me away from my assigned post (we went outside to talk for a few minutes) and was certainly about to ravish me (we kissed) when Jason and Miguel turned up.

Did they pale in horror? Did they yell "Unhand that damsel?!" No, they waited until Stone left, and teased me a little, but basically did not seem to think my honor had been besmirched. (I have to admit I kind of enjoyed my old crush seeing that I'd grown up.)

The point is, nobody makes a big deal of us except Uncle Mac.

July 25, 1994

Ask and it shall be given. Suddenly . . . a window of opportunity! (Another window—uh-oh.) Uncle Mac to go out of town on a case for a few days; I'm to stay with Tiffany and Sean. I resent this and say so but shut up when I see definite possibilities. . . .

July 26, 1994

All set. Asked permission to go on a hike and a picnic with friends from school. Tiff and Sean, after dutiful questions, said okay. It did alarm me a little, how easy it was to deceive them. Tiny little specks of guilt, but I could swat them, like mosquitos. Isn't a half-truth somewhat better than a whole lie? The hike and picnic are true. So the friend is singular and not from school? It means Stone and I can have an entire blissful day together, just us, with nobody in our face.

August 1, 1994

Nobody but some bikers and a bear. Oh, God, why does everything we try to do just to be together wind up such a disaster?! Helicopters and bloodhounds and people sick with terror (especially me) and the wrath of Mac about to descend, all because we wanted to take a simple walk in the woods? Was that bear a metaphor? Is the universe sending us a message? I'm sure Uncle Mac thinks so, and frankly, I'd rather face that bear again than him.

So beautiful. That purple misty time of almost evening. We sit by my fire (proudly made with three matches; the city boy was impressed) knowing no one will come and make pronouncements. No one—no one knows we're here. I make us pigs-in-blankets that taste like heaven. We are allowed the longest, most luxurious conversation we've ever had.

35

Some things I don't want to think about: Will I be here after next year (my senior year)? College? I don't mention the Yale dream; he might feel put down. Does he have plans? No, I'm the planner. He likes to "hang loose," take life's surprises. (So why is he asking where I'll be?? How come he cares?)

I wonder if I was a surprise to his life. I tentatively ask re G.E.D. He doesn't seem put off, but I don't press. Sonny has "opportunities" for him. I feel a chill, but let it go. I don't have answers about my future. Why should I have opinions about his?

He has kissed me a few times today, long and wonderful, but I can feel him being careful, as if it would be too easy to take advantage of the situation. (It probably would. God, if kisses can do that much to you, what is the rest of it like?)

Still, we are content and close and feeling simply happy when we hear the low roaring sound. Cycles, Stone says, sure they won't come into the woods this far. Anyway, it's time for us to pack up.

We start to smother the fire and hear footsteps. Two biker hoods, huge and mean-looking, swagger into the clearing. Stone pulls me behind him. One sneers and makes an ugly remark at me. Without a beat, Stone lands a heavy punch on him and decks him, at the same time yelling at me to run. How can I leave him, two against one? But he pushes me. I run into the woods but turn and can see them both going after him. He's amazing, hitting back hard at both of them, but one picks up a log and hits him in the head. He falls and is totally still.

They go through his pockets for money and start off but one of them spots me. I run as far and as fast as I can, just wanting to find a way, a trail or something. Get out and get some help for Stone. Now I am running in the dark.

I must have tripped and fallen and knocked myself out, because when I woke everything was fuzzy. Rustling sounds and little growls and when I could make things out, about ten feet away from me, helping himself to whatever is left in my backpack, by tearing it to shreds, was this humongous bear.

I play dead. Not because I'm smart; I _feel_ dead. Done-for. The bear finishes the marshmallows, tosses the pack, and ambles off. I wait and make a break for it. Not long enough; he's after me. I jump into the first tree big enough and climb. The bear stands at the bottom and shakes it!

Either my prayers are answered or the bear gets bored and finally moves off. I am paralyzed and still praying, not just for me but for Stone, who I picture lying there passed out as bear-bait. I am still there when the rescue party finds me in the morning.

Later

Uncle Mac was how you'd expect, only worse, and Tiffany couldn't defuse him by trying to take the blame. He was mad at her and Sean, but he was ten times madder at me—not so much for nearly getting killed, as for lying.

But my brush with death must have made me bold: I said right to his face that I'd do it again, because no matter how many rules he makes, he can't stop two people who want to from being together!

Mac looked tired and spent, as though something he'd been running after had gotten away, and he just didn't have any more energy or any more ways to trap it. After seeming exactly the same age for as long as I'd known him, he suddenly looked older. But I am older, too, and I pointed that out as the problem. "So when," he said, "am I supposed to stop caring? When am I supposed to stop loving you?"

It was the first time he'd said he loved me in a long while, and maybe the first that I'd believed it. I could see, and he admitted it, that what was underneath all this blustering and bellowing and making of edicts was that he was scared.

God, is everybody scared about everything, most of the time? Is that what makes you adult and responsible?

Even later, same date
Uncle Mac Recants

Stone is right. Life has some amazing surprises. Like Uncle Mac going to get him at Sonny's, and inviting him to dinner to discuss our "options." (First I knew I had any.)

Stone is quiet and cool as Mac starts out by dissing his relationship with Sonny and his "unstructured, unfocused life." (Mac admits it's not his business, except it is, because of me.)

Then he astounds us both by offering Stone a job at the Outback. I am elated, briefly, but Stone declines politely: he likes the job he has, thank you. (I'm disappointed, but I have to admire him for this.)

Now that he can say "I gave the kid a chance and he blew it," I expect Mac to wash his hands of Stone, but he doesn't. He goes on to remind us of our history of getting into trouble together (like we needed this) and asks what he's supposed to do to be able to sleep at night instead of worrying about me.

At this point something breaks open in Stone. His voice shakes: Mac will never understand how he felt when he couldn't find me last night. He knows what can happen "out there" and he'll do anything in his power not to let it happen to me.

More emotion than I've ever seen Stone show publicly, followed by a miracle: it reaches Uncle Mac. I see the actual instant it sinks into his brain that Stone truly cares about me and that when he says he'll protect me, he means it.

So Mac makes a proposal: in exchange for his lifting the ban on us (like it had worked) he will get an accounting of where we are at any given time and what we are doing. The idea is to re-establish trust in both directions.

It is "an offer we couldn't refuse." Stone and I are jubilant. Mac is still worried. What do we do now?

Souvenirs of ordeal which produced miracle. Too bad it's not a bear-skin.

August 7, 1994

Bark from "the tree"

This is so weird. I have seen Stone every day for a week, mostly not for very long, and always in accordance with The Agreement, but there we are, speaking in normal voices instead of whispering, not always keeping one eye out for fear of discovery, making sure there's an open window close by, not waiting breathlessly for the next time we might be able to connect. I almost miss it. It had a certain flavor.

I don't think it is coincidental, though, that Uncle Mac seems to need me for longer hours at the Outback and that he is hounding me about sending for college catalogs. The Agreement did not include his actually liking Stone.

August 12, 1994

Believe it! Genuine, romantic, guardian-approved First Date: Dinner at the Outback! (Was Stone being funny or careful?) We ate bouillabaisse and crème brulee and MELISSA MANCHESTER CAME AND SANG US <u>OUR</u> SONG: "IN A PERFECT WORLD." (Stone cool, tried not to be impressed she's an old friend of Mac's, but failed. Sees Mac in new light.).

> *"Sometimes it seems so unfair*
> *Like the universe just doesn't care*
> *That it could tear our two souls apart."*

Used to be our favorite lines. I'd break up every time I heard them. But the Universe seems to be on our side now, and the song, while romantic and beautiful, is way too sad to be ours.

OUTBACK

Desserts

Pecan Pie: à la mode

Mocha Chocolate Mousse

Hazelnut Torte

Crème Brulee

Surely the sexiest dessert known to man, especially when fed to each other with my uncle turning green across the room.

August 13, 1994

Still glowing. Scared to notice how good the future looks. A lot to figure out and a lot to resolve, but mainly so much to experience together.

Maybe I'm beginning to change in <u>Stone's</u> direction: I'm getting to kind of like the surprises of life.

August 15, 1994

I taught Stone how to roller-blade! He was immediately great at it (he is incredibly naturally graceful) but he got tired fast. He says he is out of shape from spending all his spare time with me instead of working out. I said he looked pretty good to me.

He said he liked my shape, too.

It occurred to me then that in all this time I still haven't seen him without a shirt. I must figure out an activity where this might happen naturally. Hmm.

August 19, 1994

I wanted to go to the beach, but city boy didn't feel like it, so I suggested we butter up Uncle Mac by doing some accumulated yard work at the house. (I am going to ask him if we can go to Lollapalooza in September.)

I swear the matter of shirtlessness was nowhere in my con-scious mind. However, this did occur "naturally" about midway between his trimming the hedge and my edging the lawn. (That is, it occurred with Stone, not with me!) He matter-of-factly unbut-toned his shirt, took it off, and used it to wipe the sweat off him-self. I was still wearing a rather modest halter outfit (rather, not entirely) and I kept it on, despite a sudden inclination to rip every-thing off and pull him behind the hydrangeas. I know it is still too soon but I am starting to wonder when.

August 26, 1994

It has been less than a month since the bear and our emancipation, and during that time we have:

Seen five movies (of which my favorite was "Shawshank Redemption" and his "Forrest Gump"—you'd think it would be the opposite, wouldn't you?).

Taken a total of fourteen walks together (day and night). Attempted basketball, which he insists is a great outlet for hostility. (Maybe I don't have any because I'm really lousy at it— even Stone agrees.)

Played: Badminton. (More my speed; he thinks it's lame.) Croquet. (Honest, yes, Stone, making cracks the whole time that I'm trying to civilize him. He beat me.) Many arcade games, including pinball, which I really love. (It feels somehow metaphorical, but I'm not sure of what.) We have also talked a lot, and not talked. We went to a symphony concert in the park (Stone fell asleep but swears he liked the music) and a Melody Tent performance of "West Side Story." (He caught the Romeo and Juliet reference right away.)

I tried to introduce him to some of my favorite authors but he's just not a reader. He says he's lazy. I think he just never got into it.

Obviously we are making up for lost time. Mac watches it all with this jaded look, clearly hoping it will be over soon. Ha. This is the best summer I ever had.

THE SHAWSHANK REDEMPTION
Showing at: 01:10
TUESDAY   6: 25.95

Admit: 1 BG MA $7.00
Control: 029669 Issued: 8: 30

FORREST GUMP
Showing at: 01:10
TUESDAY   8: 15.95

Admit: 1 BG MA $7.00
Control: 029669 Issued: 8: 00

MELODY TENT
Port Charles, N.Y.

WEST SIDE STORY

FANTASY RIDES
LASINO ARCADE
PORT CHARLES, NY

832817 5

THREE POINTS

WORLD TICKET SYNDICATE ••• (C) 285 **D**

FANTASY R
LASINO ARC
PORT CHARLE

5

THREE PO

WORLD TICKET SYNDIC

SUMMER 1994

August 29, 1994

There is no way to avoid it: eight days until school starts.
What? Me—star of academe, probable valedictorian of the class of
'95—unthrilled at the thought? Before Stone, I loved this time of
year, because it signified going back to the area where I am best in
control. ("Unconnected," maybe, but still in control.) I guess control isn't the trip it used to be.

Not that I'm expecting my grades to slip. Heaven forbid! If they did, you can bet the Agreement would be ripped up in front of my face and thrown to the wind.

The problem is I just don't want to deal with trying to integrate it all: Stone-life, school-life, Uncle Mac-life, and future-life (planning for it— college, etc.). I know there has to be a way to make it all work, but I can't stand having to spend the time and energy figuring it out, because that takes away from the time available for living it.

And I want to spend every bit of that time I can with Stone.

August 30, 1994

It is weird to me that Uncle Mac, who is so hot on the subject of my education, can't seem to grasp that being with Stone is an education in itself. (Oh, wow, can you hear him react to that one?)

What I mean is, sociologically my perspective has broadened. Also philosophically. It doesn't mean I have changed my basic values, it means I can comprehend the reality of someone else's point of view. Someone coming from, excuse the cliché, a different world. Even the fact that there are different worlds out there, and that some of them need changing and that is the job of civilization.

It is an outrage that kids can be "on the street" and that it actually might be better than the awful reality of their home liv es. The world is full of outrages: war and pestilence (think AIDS, for God's sake) and hunger and environmental devastation and people abusing one another.

That people are able to connect with love at all is a miracle.

43

We have, and it is.

August 31, 1994

Not to diminish the above, but here's a mini-miracle: Mac said yes to Lollapalooza! Is this because he is softening towards Stone? Aware of our increasing maturity, responsibility? No, it's because of some perverse, reverse nostalgia for Woodstock (the regret he didn't get there).

Whatever. I may turn out to have a life after all.

September 20, 1994

I knew it was too good to be true. There is no room for us on the Lollapalooza busses! I refuse to believe this. I will not accept it. We will get there if I have to take Desperate Measures.

I suggest we hitch a ride, and my suddenly straight-arrow boyfriend says, no, Mac would kill us! I suggest we drive, and Stone Cates, defender of law and order, reminds me I can't drive legally and Mac won't allow me in a car at night with him, anyway.

Stupidly, I tell Uncle Mac the problem, hoping he'll soften up about our driving. (Stone really did an awfully good job on that hedge.) But noooo. Instead he offers a brilliant solution: HE WILL DRIVE US THERE!

Right. "This is my boyfriend, Stone Cates, and this is my guardian, Uncle Mac Scorpio, defender of my virtue." And suddenly there is this empty circle all around us like we have the plague or something.

Grateful as I am (and I am, for the thought, as well as appalled), I convince Mac he is too badly needed at the Outback on Friday.

September 23, 1994

The Universe has turned again. I should have known when my plan actually shocked Stone: "And Mac thinks I'm the bad influence." Unfortunately this didn't make me think, it only made me giggle.

So, because he's willing to do about anything for me these days (so sweet) I talked him into diverting Mac's attention while I

44

borrowed the extra set of keys to Mac's car and borrowed the car itself from the Outback parking lot, knowing Mac wouldn't come for it until after closing and Stone knows how to turn back the odometer (a skill acquired in his previously less than lawful life). I figured Smashing Pumpkins was worth the risk.

Well, they would have been. Dumb skunk. Why didn't its mother teach it to look both ways? Stone and I are cruising along, well within the speed limit, on our way to truly belonging to our generation, when there is this <u>thud</u>—and in about two seconds a smell such as you've never smelled, at least to this degree, pervades Mac's car.

Smashing Pumpkins has been replaced by a smashed skunk. I suppose I should feel sorry for it but it's probably ruined my life, so I guess we're even.

I have just bathed and washed my hair three times in tomato juice. (Good thing Uncle Mac buys in case lots. A habit, I guess from owning a restaurant.) I was afraid he'd walk in on me trying to wash my clothes, so I wrapped them in three trash bags and hid them outside.

Horrible thought: what if there are skunks somewhere in the area and they are attracted to the smell and there are suddenly half a dozen horny skunks in the backyard. . . . Stop it! I am getting carried away by fear and guilt. I'd better go pretend I'm asleep. No way can I face Mac tonight.

It took eleven cans!

8 *Varieties*®

Tomato Juice

from concentrate

NET 46 FL. OZ. (1 QT. 14 OZ.) 1.36 LITERS

September 26, 1994

At least I didn't have to tell a direct lie. (I've become superb at half-truths.) I said we never got to the concert (true), I said we couldn't get on the bus (true), and when Uncle Mac voiced his thory that we'd used the car and hit a skunk, I said how much I really resent his suspicions (how true, even when they're warranted).

Of course when he left the Outback last night and got into his car he computed the full truth fairly quickly, the alternative being that a skunk (rare occurrence in the neighborhood) committed suicide somewhere near the air-conditioning duct. I worked up some righteous indignation (saved up from earlier incidents) and said I'd better get to school because if my grades dropped he'd really make my life miserable (true).

Later, 8:30 P.M.

Something intensely weird is going on. Uncle Mac, furious this morning, did a complete 180 tonight, apologized to Stone and me, treated us to dinner, plus gave each of us a copy of the new Smashing Pumpkins CD.

He says this is to make up for jumping to conclusions this morning. Went on and on about how unfair he's been and showered us (yes, Stone, too) with these effusive compliments till it got really embarrassing.

He now insists that if I tell him I don't know how the skunk smell got into the car, he believes me, because the pact we made is based on truth and trust, and after all, "skunks happen."

I feel like a skunk myself.

Later, midnight

Now I feel worse. Not just guilty and rotten, but so bad for Uncle Mac that I could cry. It turns out Felicia is pregnant–with Frisco's baby! How could such a thing happen? I mean, I know how it happens, I just don't know how she could let it. Good grief, she's the one handing out condoms!!

It's not like Felicia is promiscuous or was unfaithful to Uncle Mac. In fact, he told me, in a moment of candor I'd just as soon have skipped, that he'd sent her after Frisco the night he cancelled the wedding. (Guess it's obvious what happened then.)

The most awful thing is there was some question for a while as to whether it was Frisco's baby or Uncle Mac's. And I guess Uncle Mac really and truly hoped it was his. Uncle Mac wants to be a father. I didn't even realize that. He wants to be a father to a baby. I can't blame him. Babies are innocent, and they don't lie.

October 10, 1994

Item from a far corner of my life: my Yale application. I applied for Early Decision, in the spring. (Mentioned it only in passing to Stone, who acted unthreatened.) Now I'd almost like to cancel and apply to Port Charles U., but can't quite do it. Last year when Mac and I went on that college-scouting expedition, Yale was it, hands-down. There was something about the feeling there that spoke scholarship without stuffiness.

Moreover, with Mac being as nice as he still is, I guess I owe him that much. Doesn't mean, on the far-out chance Yale accepts me, that I _have_ to go.

Still, wouldn't Anna and Robert Scorpio have loved their daughter getting an Ivy League education! Not that they were snobs, but they wanted excellence for me. Why am I kidding myself? I want excellence for me. I can't pass it off on Mac or my parents. Except as they raised me to want it.

Does Stone represent excellence? Not in Uncle Mac's book, I know. (Nice as he's being, I don't think he likes Stone any better.) But it's not Uncle Mac's book we're reading here. In mine Stone is the most excellent thing in my life.

Does Early Decision _really_ have to mean Final Decision?

October 12, 1994

Happy Birthday To Me

Stone's gift: a small stuffed grinning brown bear, to which he has affixed a sign made on Sonny's computer: You Should Have Seen the One That Got Away.

Very funny, honey.

(He told me later he really wanted to get me a skunk, but was afraid Mac would make the connection.)

47

October 13, 1994

Uncle Mac's gift was so outrageously generous I cringed. Spelling it out here makes me feel worse. State-of-the-art stereo set-up for my room. Why did he do this? I had a perfectly decent CD boom-box.

My guilt keeps ticking. Stone has offered to come clean, but I just can't take the chance. The truth wouldn't set us free, it would just tear us apart. Give Mac the ultimate upper hand.

Meanwhile I am being so good I make myself sick. The old me is risen and she gives me a pain.

Well, at least it's peaceful at home.

October 15, 1994

In order to Experience the Fall (and in search of Mac-approved activities) I took Stone apple-picking, a concept totally foreign and somewhat suspicious to him. I.e., he knew intellectually that they grow on trees but had never entirely accepted it.

Well, where did you think apples came from?

Dumpsters, he grins.

(Every once in a while he comes out with something like that, just matter-of-factly, and I get this searing pain through me, seeing him in my head at twelve, scrounging around in alleys for food and warmth.)

We go way to the back of the orchard where the apples are supposed to be the sweetest. (Most people don't want to go that far or wait that long, so the fruit's allowed to ripen longer on the trees.) We curl up together under the shade of one. I offer him an apple but he says no, not yet.

October 31, 1994

I must be some kind of exhibitionist: I love this being a Couple.

I love us being seen together and looking at each other the way we can't help looking. (People notice us, amused, touched, sometimes wistful.)

I don't even mind being teased about it. I feel this weird kind of pride. This wonderful hot sweet funny cool guy is Mine. As much as anybody can be anybody's in a preliminary sort of relationship. Preliminary to what? That, as Hamlet says, is the question.

I refuse to think beyond today.

November 1, 1994

I take that back: it's not "preliminary." It is what it is right now and it is, as Stone would say, "choice."

November 10, 1994

Stone off on an L & B appearance (he's going to sell T-shirts and help keep the groupies off "the talent" –Eddie Maine and the Idle Rich). I'm trying very hard not to worry about who will keep the groupies off of <u>him</u>.

A year, two months, and a week after I met him, looking at Stone, thinking about Stone still makes me feel weak and slightly crazy. And wanting to bare my claws at anyone with the same idea.

November 14, 1994

I have a number of stupid questions about sex that I can't ask anyone. If I asked Felicia she would immediately make assumptions again and she would be wrong (unfortunately). If I asked

Brenda she would laugh her head off. (I laugh, too, when I think of them, but that doesn't give me any answers.)

These questions aren't physiological (or obviously I could research them) and are not ideological (or I could probably figure out what I think). They are more logistical—nitty-gritty kinds of things. They aren't even as sophisticated as who does what to whom first. (There I am willing to be surprised.) They are as dumb as how do you get your clothes off gracefully.

I mean it is very nice to think about his removing them, but even then there are awkward elements. What if he has trouble with your bra? Do you help?

When you see these explicit scenes in movies there is always a fade-out just at the point where it would get clumsy. Then they fade back in and the principals are unclothed on some horizontal surface with a cover of some sort delicately draped. (Or not, depending on the rating.) One way or the other, you probably didn't see them take their shoes off.

Shoes might not be a problem if you're wearing something simple that slips off sexily, but then you have the problem of socks or pantyhose, both of which are a little ridiculous. Or what if you're wearing shoes that have to untie—maybe even tennis shoes? (Granted you probably wouldn't wear tennis shoes to have sex, but what if you didn't plan on it that day when you got dressed?)

It must have been a lot easier in the Old Days when you got married first and came out of the bathroom in a peignoir. (I know this from fifties movies on TNT.)

Then there is the further problem of Protection. How and when does this occur? Obviously things have to have progressed to a reasonable point before this can happen. So it seems to me some-time in the throes of passion everything has to come to a sudden halt while he gets this dumb thing on. Doesn't this break the mood?

Well, I suppose it has to do with Felicia's statement—that pas-sion can be overwhelming. Maybe you're so into it you just don't notice. Clearly people are managing. But it is this kind of thing that prevents me from having an adequate fantasy life.

November 24, 1994

It's going to be a weird Thanksgiving. Not exactly Over the River and Through the Woods to Grandmother's House.

I'm going to the house of estranged but still married friends, along with my uncle and his ex-fiancée, bringing my boyfriend, disliked and unapproved of by my uncle. Should be a real joy. The idea, I think, is to give everyone (especially the two small kids) the illusion of Family. Kevin Collins will be there, too, which is a good thing. Maybe he'll give us a group rate.

But am I thankful? God, yes.

Though Stone and I operate under this uneasy truce with Uncle Mac, we are still together. (A fact that makes Uncle Mac even more uneasy.) Ever since the Night of the Skunk we have been excruciatingly truthful with him about where we are, though we may occasionally "sin by omission" regarding what we are doing.

Actually we are not doing anything that couldn't be featured in a PG movie. Maybe even G-rated. Not because we don't want to, because I think both of us do (God, I hope so), but we are still proceeding with caution.

Sometimes I feel very ready and wonder if Stone just doesn't find me exciting enough. Then again, sometimes I look back at those "criteria" I wrote months ago and think, even though they were a kind of academic avoidance at the time, maybe there is something to them.

I'm also aware we have already met a certain number of them.

I started to write about Thanksgiving and ended up writing about sex again (or the lack thereof). Whatever happened to my intellect? (I guess it's been put in its place.)

Later, 10 P.M.

Some Thanksgiving! I'm not thankful, I'm furious!

"We gathered together," ready to sublimate our various frustrations in food, all of us well aware that whatever our problems, our lives are remarkably good. Especially Stone, who is probably the only one among us who's ever been genuinely hungry.

Stone and I had been hanging out in the kitchen, trying to be

51

helpful to Bobbie (and giving us a chance to make out a little—big deal). Uncle Mac came in to get us for dinner and got on my case about being rude, staying apart from the other guests (though at this point he was keeping me from joining them).

I reminded him of the terms of The Agreement, which did not prohibit a little innocent making out in a friend's kitchen. He was already in a bad mood and this seemed to set him off. He said that "deal" had expired about the same time as the skunk!

I was knocked, figuratively, on my butt, flailing around for a response. First I acted like I didn't remember: "What skunk?" He refreshed my memory: "The one you hit the night you borrowed my car without asking me first …?"

I felt like I'd been punched in the stomach and hit on the head at the same time. Uncle Mac had known all along. Why didn't he say anything?! Because he was "tired of yelling" at me and "wasn't getting anywhere." And this is the biggie: So he "thought of other ways" to make me regret what I'd done." !!!

In other words all the niceness and kindness and good cheer and all those compliments over two solid months since the end of September were designed to make me (and Stone) squirm! They were a conscious, chosen manipulation of our guilt. How could he? How could he? It's the rottenest, most cruel thing anyone's ever done to me, and I told Mac so.

He then proceeded (after refusing Kevin's attempt to mediate, Thanksgiving dinner getting cold on the table) to lay me out in front of everyone there about my irresponsibility and dishonesty and general crummy behavior and I yelled back about his pathetic need to control my life—when all of a sudden Lucy Coe walks in with a live duck!!!

Stone and I took advantage of the resulting chaos to escape. I wanted to go back to his place (Sonny and Brenda are off in Puerto Rico on L & B business), but maybe he was afraid we'd lose control, because he said no, so we went to Kelly's. Ruby keeps the place open on Thanksgiving so that Lost Souls have a place to go. We ate turkey sandwiches and fit right in.

Thanksgiving—before blow-up!

December 1, 1994

Like-a-morgue time again at the house. I thought maybe Uncle Mac would start invoking the ban on Stone (not that I would have paid attention) but I suppose that would have required speaking to me. Speaking to each other might require both of us to apologize, and neither of us feels like it yet.

Stone has been great. He listens, never comes down on me for whining, but also never disses Mac. In fact his take on the skunk manipulation is quite different from mine: yes, he was mad at first but then he sort of thought it was funny. Like that was a clever thing for Mac to do! Maybe that's what comes of living with a sneak like Sonny Corinthos.

December 7, 1994

Sonny is back from Puerto Rico and Stone is working longer hours than he was. I wish I knew exactly what he does, but when I ask him I get the same old answers: "this and that" or "I'm Sonny's right-hand guy." I hope the right hand knows what the left one is doing. Or actually maybe I don't.

December 10, 1994

I'm scared again, but I'm trying not to get crazy about it. Stone and I had plans for a simple movie and a burger tonight but when I got there he started waving around a hundred dollar bill Sonny had given him—to show me a good time(!)

I didn't want to squash his Up mood, but I couldn't help asking what was going on. I know L & B hasn't made any money yet, and the blues club Sonny's partnering with Luke Spencer isn't even open. Stone said he didn't know exactly, but something "big" was happening for Sonny, and he was going to be a part of it.

I couldn't cover how this made me feel, and he was all reassurance that somehow or other Frank Smith's death made everything alright. I am unreassured: Frank Smith was, everyone knows, lord of the gangsters.

If he's talking about what I think he's talking about, it is definitely not alright for Stone to be anywhere near it, but if I make too much of it now, I'll never get him away from it. I'm afraid he's so loyal to Sonny he'll walk away from me first.

Still, basically what I see here is a healthy ambition to make something of himself. He said as much: that when I go to college I'll meet guys who are "going places" and he doesn't expect to spend his life pumping gas or something. I think this is a good sign. (I also like what it implies!) I'd tell Uncle Mac (about Stone's ambition, not the rest of it), only we're still hardly speaking.

December 12, 1994

Stone and I went Christmas shopping yesterday. He is still tossing money around like crazy, says Sonny gave him a big raise. I tense, but he assures me it's legit: he's going to be in charge of valet parking for the club. The first chance he's ever had to "run" something. It is kind of touching to watch him feel successful. It's so interesting, because I can't imagine how it would feel—to assume you wouldn't be.

I've never been given any doubt about being successful in life. (Other things I have doubts about, but not that.) I was raised, first by Grandma Filomena and then by my parents, then Mac, to know I had brains, I had support, all I had to do was use them and I'd be fine.

What would it be like to be fighting, not for good grades or good conduct stars, but for food and a place to sleep? To not even consider the possibility of anyone loving you?

I bought Maxie a wonderful sort of sculpture kit that has all these different bright plastic shapes that you can move around and connect and build weird neat things. Stone liked it so much I went back today and bought him one! I hope he's not insulted. Nobody can give him back a childhood, but at least he can have some fun.

It's okay, Michael Stone Cates. You are loved. You are loved. You are loved now.

General Hospital Pediatrics Party. I'm behind Santa Tony here in my elf costume. Stone wore biker jacket, refusing to play, but once he gave out one present to a kid he was hooked and really got into it!

January 6, 1995

It's so strange that sometimes what you intend to happen doesn't, but something better happens. Well, almost. (Soon.)

It started with my acceptance from Yale.

I don't think I've actually <u>experienced</u> that yet, because so much happened around it. But, hey, that's okay, because Uncle Mac experienced it for me. And almost ruined my life in the process. (Please, please, couldn't he get one of his own??)

Right before Justus Ward's victory party (for winning the city council seat) Uncle Mac hands me this large fat envelope from Yale. He's sure it's an acceptance because rejections come in thin envelopes. I feel an actual stab of fear that he is right.

I try to put off opening it, but he is way too excited, so I do, and it is: "We are pleased to inform you . . ." They're pleased; what am I?

No doubt about Mac, though. He is jumping up and down, happily whooping it up, when he finally notices I am not. How come, he wonders. I actually have to spell it out for him: STONE.

He then proceeds to have a cow over my even thinking of this as a conflict. The Ivy League beckons, I must go forth, and to hell with the best relationship of my life.

I mention another option: Port Charles University. He has a second cow.

I point out that he's constantly telling me I lack maturity and responsibility. Maybe I'm not even ready. He makes it clear that I will be struck responsible and mature the moment I leave Stone in the dust.

I call him on his constant scapegoating of Stone: it rains, it's Stone's fault; world hunger, it's Stone's fault, etc. Of course I don't have a mind of my own—and that's Stone's fault, too.

At the party, <u>my</u> acceptance is apparently <u>Mac's</u> news to tell. He babbles it to Tiffany and Sean, who are thrilled for me. Stone arrives and I take him aside, knowing this isn't the time or place. I intend to tell him later, alone, approach it carefully, with lots of reassurance.

But we're hanging out with Jason and Keesha Ward, when Uncle Mac blazes by like a neon sign, drops "Robin's good news," and goes on his way, leaving Stone reeling and me mortified. Stone tries hard to congratulate me along with Jason and Keesha and then just walks away. I go after him and he wonders when (and if, I guess) I intended to tell him.

I take him back to the house to explain. Forget the rules—if Mac hadn't been so insensitive, I wouldn't have to break them. (I can't help it, though: I love the look on Stone's face that says how much he doesn't want me to leave.)

I tell him, and I mean it with all my heart, that if he asks me to stay, I will tell Yale no thank you.

He won't do that, of course, and is starting to sound like Mac, saying how different we are and how he's a bad influence on me. I don't buy this, and get the feeling he's avoiding something. Finally he admits it: he loves me.

Stone loves me.

Stone loves me. He said it out loud. (He's been acting like it for a while, and I didn't think it was an issue that he hadn't said it, until he did and the joy hit me.)

But here is the problem: just like me, everyone he's ever loved, he's lost.

I touch his face and tell him no way, can't happen, he won't lose me. Ever. I look in his eyes, see his doubt—not of me, but of anything, anything at all lasting. And in that moment I realize there are no guarantees. It may not be up to me. With love, loss is always possible.

All I know is that this time, right now, belongs to us together. And it could ultimately be the only thing we ever really have. Everything is moving, spinning, changing so fast. So before the Universe turns around again, I want to make love. I want to make love with him while we still can. Now.

Stone is so sweet: am I sure? "Making love is a serious step, Robin." (This the man Mac knew would take advantage of me.)

Those criteria I worked out so carefully float by my conscious-ness, and I realize the only criterion is being clear they don't matter at all.

He kisses me in a new way—as though for once he doesn't plan to stop. Frantic, urgent, dizzying. We are closer than we've ever been. I'm more and more certain this is absolutely right . . . and Stone pulls away. We can't, he says. We don't have protection.

I feel like he's slapped me.

I am so desperate I don't care. I know he's been tested for HIV (Sonny made him when he pulled him off the street). I know there hasn't been anyone else for a long time. God knows I have no history. Pregnancy? It can't happen just like that, can it?

Mac's right. I am irresponsible. Stone is the one who says no.

I wonder out loud if he just doesn't want to—with me. He gives me a look that makes me know better. He says it doesn't mean we're not going to. Just not tonight.

The one thing I'm sure of is it will be soon.

It's almost a postscript that Mac comes home as Stone's leaving. He tries to throw a fit, but neither Stone nor I care.

He tells me I'm grounded. I say no, I'm not. He is shocked into silence. I am way past being grounded.

January 12, 1995

I think it's going to be Friday night—the night "Luke's" opens.

Of course when Stone came over to the Outback to invite me to the opening (they are featuring B. B. King!), Mac right away said no, I was still grounded. I didn't argue the generality with him, because I wanted to argue the specific.

Uncle Sean happened to be there and tried to help, offering to come along with Tiffany as chaperones. After all, it would be a major event. (He should only know.)

Mac said for that matter why didn't he go along, which as far as I was concerned trashed the evening for us, so I said forget it, I won't go. Mac said suit yourself and went off.

But Stone looked at me, with this wonderful look of promise and said he knew a way we could see B. B. King and be alone together—watch it on the video set-up in Sonny's apartment . . .

Perfect. Mac will be downstairs at the club, so he won't know I'm not home. Poetically perfect.

Here's to independence and womanhood. God, I love Stone so much, and I'm so glad I do.

Five days.

January 18, 1995

Luke's Club won't open Friday. It was fire-bombed last night—and riddled with bullets—apparently by guys who were after Sonny.

Mac was the one who showed me the story in the paper. He wasn't exactly gloating, but he didn't mind saying "I told you so." And went into his refrain of "Sonny Corinthos is bad news." Subtext: So is anyone who associates with him. So is Stone.

I am scared again, more than ever (I never really stopped, just kept stomping it down). Not scared about Stone, but for him.

When I said thank God he hadn't been there, he said he wished he had been—when Sonny needed him! He's that loyal. So grateful to Sonny for saving his life that he's willing to turn around and risk it for him.

Stone says the hit was about "old stuff" and that Sonny's "taking care of it." All I can remember is Duke telling my mother over and over that he was "out of it." The only way Duke finally got "out of it" was they killed him.

Duke never told my mother the truth when she'd ask questions —not to hide it from us, but to keep us safe. Knowledge isn't power with the mob; it's danger.

This is what I told Stone: as frightened as I am about this, I won't ask you any questions. Because I never, ever want you to lie to me.

This doesn't seem like a solution, but what else can I do? What else could my mother do? She loved him.

January 31, 1995

You do what you can, I guess, and sometimes it's only bringing chicken soup. Stone has the flu: fever, horrible sore throat, aches all over.

He's being stubborn about working instead of resting (this is the guy Mac thinks is a deadbeat), but I can't seem to stop him. Anyway, he'd better get over it fast, because the repairs on Luke's are almost finished and they are planning to open next week—with B. B. King—and Stone and I have a date. . . .

February 4, 1995, 3 A.M.

Harborside Motel

. . . And sometimes what you want to happen really does.

Michael Stone Cates is sleeping beside me. His breathing is gentle, makes almost no sound. It's quiet here except for the hum of a few cars on the highway overpass, a little way down on the road.

The Harborside Motel is not near the harbor or really beside anything. It does not at first look meet my early hope for a "reasonably romantic situation," but I guess romantic must be in the eyes of the people in love who need to be alone and away from anything chasing them or stopping them.

I took hold of my life; I took command of my body. I wanted to give it to Stone, and I did. And I'm more sure than ever that it was the exactly right thing to do, exactly now.

I am amazingly happy.

The fact of this finally actually happening did <u>not</u> have to do with Uncle Mac. It was not an act of rebellion or anger. It was an act of love and had only to do with Stone and me.

That it occurred here, in what the travel books refer to as an "economy class" motel, <u>did</u> have to do with Uncle Mac, who broke through the door of Sonny's apartment last night during Luke's opening and found us half-dressed and on our way. He acted like I was sick and what we were doing was dirty.

It's hard to forgive him for that, but it doesn't matter, because I'm not and it wasn't. He tried to trash something beautiful, but he didn't manage.

What he did was make it possible for us to be completely free and unafraid, the way it should have been in the first place.

No one knowing where we were. No one to judge or prevent. Letting us be not frantic and furtive, but deliberate and slow and careful. Allowing for shyness, forgiving of awkwardness, the clumsiness I was afraid of. (Shoes? I honestly don't remember.)

Stone undressed me as if he was unwrapping a gift—a package marked fragile, something amazing and precious. It was the first time I ever actually felt beautiful. Stone so gentle and sure. So incredibly close. Complete.

I wanted it to happen and it did. I wanted it to be with him and it was.

I feel as though I finally belong to myself. The paradox is I also belong, totally, to Stone.

Later, 10 A.M., Home

I came home at dawn to face Uncle Mac. Stone awoke as I was dressing to leave, wanted to come with me, but I knew I had to do it alone. Needed to stand without protection and tell my guardian that I'd done the thing he most feared, and I was fine. Better than fine. Whole, adult, and confident of my own judgment.

I wanted to assure Mac that he hadn't betrayed my parents' trust. That he had taken care of me until it was time for me to take care of myself. That when he'd accused me of making the worst mistake of my life, he was simply wrong. The only thing he was right about was that I couldn't take it back.

I didn't get to say much of that because he was still so angry. I guess nothing makes you angrier than feeling helpless.

At that point, and probably a good thing, Felicia arrived, just back from Texas. Mac immediately announced what had happened and pretty much turned me over to her before he could have a heart attack. Then he left the house.

I didn't mind Felicia knowing, though I minded Mac telling. She was very kind and supportive and non-condescending—seemed to realize I'd made a choice.

After she'd made sure I'd been responsible (used protection, found out that Stone was HIV negative), she suggested I see a doctor right away and, if recommended, go on the pill, pointing out she was living proof that condoms, although <u>always</u> necessary, were not always enough. I looked at her, almost ready to deliver, and said I'd make an appointment.

And could I try, she asked, not to make this any harder on Mac than it had to be? After all, he was only trying to do what he thought a parent should do. (Exert total control over my life?)

She's sure we can work out some agreement we can both tolerate.

She's sure; I'm not. I will not agree to anything less than total freedom regarding Stone.

61

Then Brenda showed up! I was beginning to think the loss of my virginity had been the lead story in the morning news, but it turned out she'd spoken with Stone. I guess he had a right to tell her (of course he did; I don't <u>want</u> it secret), but I felt a little embarrassed—sort of over-exposed.

She wondered how I was (meaning, I guess, how "It" was), how I felt. Honestly, I couldn't even tell at that point. Even though I was sure it was the right thing to do, the actual happening seemed lost in a mass of reactions that confused, almost over-whelmed me. I was dazed.

One thing I was sure of: a lot of relief that my first time was over, and my innocence would never again be an issue. (Maybe I should get another T-shirt):

FINALLY DID IT

But I also told her what I couldn't tell Stone: that while we were the most intimate, and I was trying to be whatever it was I was supposed to be, I couldn't quite shut Mac's voice out of my head, telling me I wasn't supposed to be doing this at all.

She said it gets better with practice.

I intend to practice a lot, Mac or no Mac, until all I hear in my head are Stone's voice and mine, both saying "I love you."

Harborside MOTEL
AIR CONDITIONED

Route 278
Belleville,
N.Y. 13611
315-555-2000

SHHHH!

Do Not Disturb

February 11, 1995

What astounds me is how much it seems to have changed us both. Of course we've been changing all along, or this never would have happened. But who knew I would ever stand in front of my Uncle Mac and <u>tell</u> him where I'm going (and, by implication, what I'm doing) rather than ask.

I'm trying, per Felicia's request, not to do this in an in-your-face way. I'll always let him know where I am and when I'll be home. I know that his attempts to control my life are not

63

(strictly) neurotic, but are about the promise he made my mother and father. It is touching how important this is to him, how seriously he takes it.

And I appreciate it (at least abstractly), because I know what it did to Stone, to have no one caring. I only wish Uncle Mac could manage a little compassion. But Stone and I agree we can't change his feelings, and we won't waste energy trying. I know Stone is wonderful, and if I have my way Stone will too, eventually, and that's all that counts.

Later in the day I brought another picnic to Stone's place: more chicken soup (he's still fighting the flu), country bread, cheese and fruit, and we sat on the floor and ate it.

Something else profound I've learned from our relationship: it is very challenging to eat soup while sitting on the floor. (I notice I am a lot sillier since Stone. An improvement, I think.)

Okay, that's how I've changed. How has Stone? Here's a biggie: Stone is making plans. He told me about an ad for the summer concerts in the park and that he'd like to get tickets. (Despite the fact that he fell asleep at the last one.)

The point is, Stone, who never trusted enough in what life would hand him to make plans for anything, now assumes there will be a future. And that I will be in it. (He's right about that one.)

As soon as he said it, though, he was nervous. Like what if he got tickets and . . . well, "nothing lasts forever, Robin." Meaning I could change my mind about him.

As if.

I told him I knew from my life that nothing lasts forever, but some things are safer bets than others.

Oh, and we made love again. Brenda is right. It gets better.

February 15, 1995

Tiffany and Sean are pregnant!!! She found out (appropriately) on Valentine's Day. They are ecstatic, of course, but she is scared, too, because of the miscarriage last year. But, I tell her, just because something bad happened once doesn't mean it has to happen again. She and Uncle Sean have had their share of awful stuff to get through. I am so happy for them.

I wonder what the baby will look like. Will it be beautiful, like Tiffany, or cute, like Uncle Sean? Will it be funny, like him, or elegant, like her? Or a combination thereof? Kids are such an interesting mix.

Which can't help lead to the obvious question: what would a baby Stone and I made be like? Would his/her eyebrows be straight and on a slant, like Stone's, or curved like mine? Would she/he talk too much and think too much, like me, or watch things and seem to know from the gut, like Stone?

Not that I want to find out, in the foreseeable future.

Weird, isn't it, how what's happy news for Sean and Tiff would be disaster for me right now. I made an appointment, per Felicia's suggestion, with a gynecologist to probably get on the pill. (Just scheduling this made me feel Adult and Responsible.) But then I had to put it off a couple weeks, in the hope I'll be over the flu then.

Yes, inevitably, I guess, I got Stone's flu. Yukky throat, fever, aches, and pains. But I don't care—it was worth it. I teased him and told him he gave me the love bug.

Stone's Valentine. Who'd've thunk he'd be so traditional?

February 20, 1995

Right, Brenda: and better, and better. Despite the flu. (What's the difference, if we both have it?)

I wonder why I was so worried about knowing what I was doing making love when it is so wonderful to figure it out. Explore. Touch. Discover. Trust. Love.

So much love.

February 23, 1995

I don't get it. Does God set us up?? Why them? Why now?

Tiffany and Sean, happier than they've been in years, looking forward to what they want most in life, and randomly, stupidly, mistakenly, Uncle Sean is shot. Luke Spencer, accidental, self-defense, but what's the difference: fragments of the bullet still in his brain. Special surgery, Boston. Rehabilitation—_there_—long-term. They are leaving.

Forgive me, God, but it feels like they are leaving me.

Sorry, I know this isn't about me. But there have been so few people in my life I could count on. I didn't realize how much I counted on them.

Stone helps. He gets the picture right away: all the people lost to me. People I loved and needed. Grandma Fil, then Duke. My parents, after years, find each other again, and how long did they have—did _we_ have as a family? How long does anybody have with anybody? Even Uncle Mac, who loves me, doesn't really see me anymore. Like he's walked out on me, too.

Stone promises he won't leave my life. I know I won't leave his, ever. But suddenly the future is much more frightening. Yale, September, feels like another planet, another century. Nobody knows tomorrow. Anything can and does occur. Randomly, stupidly, mistakenly? If there's a plan it's certainly not mine.

Today I watched from a distance (because of my flu) as they wheeled Uncle Sean out, Tiffany beside him saying her good-byes and making promises—she'll write, she'll call, she'll be back with the baby. I know she means it, but right now I don't buy anybody's promises.

But I ought to be grateful, right? I _have_ to be grateful. The bullet didn't kill him. Uncle Sean can be fixed. It could just as easily have gone the other way.

March 2, 1995

If there were a relationship manual, I'd be looking under "I" for Impasse.

Stone is more stubborn than ever, and Uncle Mac, for a change, is probably right about something. Yesterday he pronounced a non-negotiable edict: I am to stay away from Luke's club.

Obviously I would have ignored that, given my new attitude, but he backed it up with information he got from Sean, and it makes a terrifying amount of sense.

This guy, Joe Scully, who is a known mobster, is hanging around Sonny—at Luke's. Apparently he had something to do with Uncle Sean's getting shot—like he set Luke Spencer up.

I didn't even argue. I remembered Duke, and I said I'd stay away. And I began thinking about it seriously, in terms of Stone. He is so crazily loyal to Sonny, and he doesn't know what I know— firsthand—about how these people operate.

So this morning I told Mac and Felicia (who was worried, too) that I was going to try to convince Stone to distance himself from all of it.

Yeah, right.

Stone was already in a bad mood when he came over, and he got progressively defensive. He even suggested that Joe Scully, who has a major record of arrests, if not convictions, could be perfectly innocent. But I could tell from his face he knew better. So, thinking to strengthen my position, I brilliantly asked Mac to lay out the facts, which he did, and added another offer for Stone to work at the Outback. Mac got interrupted, but by now Stone was mad at me for not trusting him. Also for bringing in Mac. And especially for not understanding what Sonny means to him. Well, how about what I mean to him? How about what Stone means to me? It's not about trust, it's about terror—mine—if he doesn't have the sense to have any himself.

None of that seems to matter to him. Stone said when he threw in with Sonny that it was for the long haul . . . and if I didn't like it—tough.

When I look at that written down I still can't believe it.

March 7, 1995

There is still all this tension, so when the phone rang at 4 A.M. I was sure it was the worst: Stone had been caught in a gangland shoot-out or something. But instead it was Felicia's voice, and both Mac and I (we'd picked up at the same time) were sure she was in labor.

Wrong. It was Felicia, all right, calling from General Hospital, having given birth to a baby girl on the floor at Luke's club!! See, she was waiting for Frisco (who'd promised absolutely-no-matter-what he'd be there when the baby was born). And I guess Georgie (which is now the baby's name, thanks to Maxie) didn't want to wait anymore.

They are both fine, and Felicia had the best of medical care (half the staff of GH was at Luke's to hear Mary Mae Ward sing), but both Mac and I feel kind of cheated, since most of Port Charles witnessed the event. (I guess nobody else is very worried about the presence of Joe Scully.)

Mac's over meeting the baby now. I thought I'd wait and let him have the time with them alone. It's got to be weird for him. I know deep down he wanted to be her father.

So, except for us, everyone important in Felicia's life was there . . . but Frisco. So much for promises. Confirms my theory.

You can't live on promises. You have to live on now. And right now I'm going to go over to see Stone and try again.

Afternoon, same date, Wyndham's Coffee Bar

Have I learned something about Relationships, or have I wimped out? Is Stone being straight with me? He reminded me I'd promised not to ask questions. My bright idea, remember? So that while he might not tell me everything, at least he wouldn't lie?

Still, I feel alright. Maybe this is a milestone: first major fight, and we agree to disagree. It was that or keep on fighting, which we both hate a lot.

Even though I had a very good case—including Luke sending Laura and their baby away because of Scully—it was clear Stone wasn't going to back down. I have to respect him for that. I'm still scared, but as long as we're together it'll be okay. Won't it?

I didn't know quite what to do after that, so I came here to buy a frilly pink dress for Georgie Jones, new person. I don't want to examine this impulse too carefully; I'm just going to do it. Then I'll go say welcome, Georgie, to our confusing world.

Later

She is the sweetest, most perfect thing, Georgie. In the true sense of the word: awesome. Maybe God doesn't do such a bad job after all.

March 13, 1995

3rd Period Study Hall

This has to be some kind of a record. I just had sixteen consecutive wonderful hours. (Granted I was asleep in a hotel room for maybe six of them, but still.)

Guess what, Mac. Guess what, Yale. There's a <u>real</u> world out there. And Stone's part of it. Also Brenda and Lois and Ned and the Idle Rich, and for those sixteen hours, me!

Believe it: there are live performers and live audiences made up of live fans who go crazy to get close to the performers, and I was among the chosen—chosen to work like a happy dog selling T-shirts and other Idle Rich memorabilia and to ride to Ithaca and back in the van with them.

It's not like they are the gods these fans make of them—for Pete's sake, I've known Ned Ashton half my life—but there is something so incredible about being really <u>inside</u> the business. Backstage where it's really happening. Something happens to Ned, too, when he goes onstage and becomes Eddie Maine. (No wonder Lois forgave him.) Does each of us have this wild performing person inside us?

Now I get why Stone's so hyped about the music business. And yes, he's good at it! Lois said on the way home once he gets a few more road trips under his belt she'll offer him a full-time job. Of course technically he'd still be working for Sonny, but he'd be that much farther removed from the shady side of Sonny's business. And would spend less time at Luke's. Maybe I can encourage him to get his own place.

Maybe everything.

EDDIE MAINE — Idle Rich

MAR 1 3 1995

The best part is seeing Stone so Up, so functioning, so . . . yes, proud. He loved my loving it, and I loved sharing it with him. God, we are great together.

I'd better get to English. Life continues, if not at that height. At least I didn't have to go home first and have Uncle Mac stick a pin in it. I had the Idle Rich van drop me off here—and oh, did I love the faces of my so-called friends when they saw me get out! Robin Scorpio, actually doing something Cool.

IDLE RICH
AA
PORT CHARLES
GUEST
MAR 1 3 1995

March 16, 1995

Things don't stay the same. That's what I told Lucas, though I don't know if a five-year-old can comprehend that. I'm not sure I can.

From the high of the Ithaca concert I came home to the horror of Georgie gone, and all any of us can do right now is wait for Ryan Chamberlain to call. A madman is in charge of our world at the moment. (I've suspected it all along.)

But in the middle of the madness there is something wonderful. Or really not wonderful in itself, but knowing it may change Stone's life: I am willing to bet that he is dyslexic!

He was trying to do some inventory work for Lois and having an awful time reading the papers. I offered to help and he was embarrassed, said reading was always slow for him. I pursued it a little and what he told me gave me the clue: the letters "dance" for him. Not the words and the meanings, the way they do for me sometimes, and it's a pleasure, but the letters move and change themselves as he's looking.

71

It explains so much! —His misery in school, his low opinion of himself, his unwillingness to try to finish his education. Why would he try, when deciphering every word in a book is a battle? Just thinking about it tore at my heart—a little kid laboring against letters he can't catch, nobody knowing or caring. If they noticed at all they thought he was stupid. That's what he thought. He thought the way the letters moved for him was normal, and that he just didn't have the patience or the brains to read like everyone else.

Stone's face when I told him it was a disorder—that it had a name and lots of people had it and solved it—all I can say is that he looked different from any way I've ever seen him look. Like some deep incredibly defended part of him had opened up with hope and possibility.

I don't think he quite believed me, but then Lois came in and said oh, sure, her best friend in school had had that problem—a very smart friend.

I think if he'd known where to go for help Stone would have left that minute, but none of us had any idea where to start. So I suggested he see Kevin Collins, who might be able to point him in the right direction. He'll call as soon as the mess with Georgie and Kevin's crazy brother is cleared up.

God, let it be soon!

March 21, 1995

A night of guilty home-alone bliss followed by joy and relief when Mac called: Georgie is found and safe, and Ryan Chamberlain is, this time, seriously dead.

There was a stab of conscience when I picked up the phone and heard Mac's voice, because I had to reach over Stone, sleeping in my bed, to answer.

I will now proceed to rationalize:

Life is short and, as noted frequently in these pages, extremely changeable. Opportunities for Stone and me to be together in this unhurried, wonderful way are few.

Yes, I did feel a little bad knowing everyone was out there searching for Georgie while Stone and I were eating pizza, watching videos, dancing, and yes, making love. (In my room! In my bed!) With only my assembled doll collection watching. They didn't seem too shocked. Maybe after years of my telling them my troubles, it was nice for them to see me extremely happy.

It's okay to be happy, isn't it? No matter what the circumstances, you might as well grab the good in them.

March 28, 1995

Since the magic, home-alone night (I swear my room feels different) I've been wondering how it is actually living with someone you love that much in that way.

Does it get ordinary? Do you run out of stuff to say? And what do you do when there are real conflicts, like Stone and I had last week? (It's bad enough when Uncle Mac and I walk around here avoiding each other.) This Agree to Disagree thing sounds good, but how do you live with that wad of wanting to be right stuck in your stomach?

And what about the fear? Don't you wonder all the time how and if you can keep this going? If you have a history of losing everyone you love, how can you feel safe?

Stone and I talked about this in the night, when I let myself remember what was happening with Georgie. That kind of fear brings back all the losses, like I'm about to lose every one of those people again. When I'm with Stone and I have these feelings, he holds me and I get through them. Wouldn't it be good to have the person you love right there, to hold you whenever you need it?

We made a pact that night: "No more losing people we love." Like anybody really has a choice. Still, you ought to be able to work at it. At least not lose them through carelessness or stupidity.

plastic straws

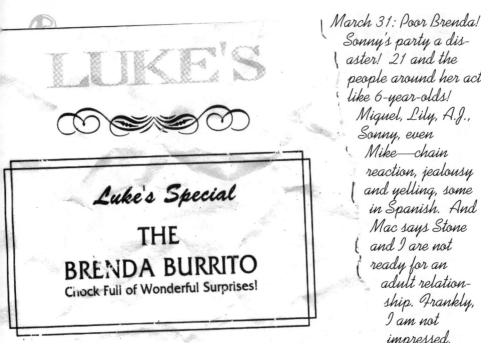

March 31: Poor Brenda! Sonny's party a disaster! 21 and the people around her act like 6-year-olds! Miguel, Lily, A.J., Sonny, even Mike—chain reaction, jealousy and yelling, some in Spanish. And Mac says Stone and I are not ready for an adult relationship. Frankly, I am not impressed.

April 4, 1995
English class

Ms. Harper droning on about Alexander Pope. The only romantic couplet I care about is Stone and me. Right this minute Stone's in Kevin Collins's office testing for dyslexia. Weird to hope someone <u>does</u> have a disorder.

Felt so much for him this morning. Stopped by to wish him luck with Kevin, and he seemed so undefended and anxious. I understand him more and more. How must it feel to grow up with everybody tearing you down instead of giving you confidence? If his family had stayed together, Stone would probably have been the black sheep anyway (like Uncle Mac!). At least on the street he learned something about his own resiliency.

I respect him and love him so much for acting on this right away. It will be an incredible relief when we find out for sure that Stone's problem has a name.

April 5, 1995

Stone much more relaxed—Kevin put him at his ease—and really eager to move with it. Tony's set up neurological tests. (No biggie—just to rule out an organic basis.)

He can't get over how nice everyone's being about this. I point out this may be because people like him, which seems to be hard for him to believe. If I never do anything else in my life, I only hope I can some day convince Michael Cates that he is worthy.

April 11, 1995

Beyond belief!! Isn't there a limit somewhere to the humiliation a parent or guardian is entitled to inflict on you?

Lois's parents, visiting from Brooklyn, came into the Outback today and her father recognized Uncle Mac right away—as "a guy" who'd been in his sporting goods store a few months ago asking "all those questions about Sonny Corinthos." Mac actually went undercover and all the way to Brooklyn to investigate my boyfriend's employer!!!

What's worse is, once he got over the surprise, Mr. Cerullo wasn't even mad—seems he understands how it is raising teenage daughters.

April 12, 1995

I was right! I was right! I was right! Stone is dyslexic.

His neurological tests came back clean—no brain tumors or anything dire about his nervous system. (I didn't even realize I was worried underneath.)

It's like a new life is beginning for him—possibilities he never thought could be there. And he says this is due to me.

Obviously this is only slightly so. He's the one who followed through; he's the one fighting to make something of himself. (As far as I'm concerned, he already is something . . . so much.)

But it feels so great to have helped make him this happy and optimistic. We are both beginning to believe in a future together, though we're shy about saying so.

We bounded into bed and made love, almost like a celebration—in such a wonderful hurry that for the first time we didn't use a condom. Stone was concerned afterward (he is so sweet), but I said I was protected against pregnancy now by the pill. (And since he's tested HIV negative, we're home free.) It really is nice to be that spontaneous—closer, freer, and all that.

Stone is amused by how eager I am all the time. Says he's created a monster. Also says he can live with it.

April 14, 1995

One year ago today Michael Stone Cates kissed me and totally changed my life.

April 20, 1995

Why us? This kind of happiness feels almost crazy; almost illegal; almost unfair to everybody else. How can I be entitled to this? What were the odds of Stone and Robin finding each other? I'm sure this euphoria won't last forever. If nothing else, Uncle Mac will make some snide comment and it will fizzle. But right now, all I can see is it's getting better and better.

Even though Stone's still wrestling with the meanest flu bug in modern history, we still can have fun and be silly together. Today I fed him ice cream spoonful by spoonful as he practiced his reading technique. Of course this didn't last too long because pretty soon we were practicing other techniques.

Am I becoming a brazen creature? Sometimes all I can think about is the Next Time. (That is, when I am not thinking about the Last Time.) To be that close, that fused. Nothing between us. Not clothes, not space, not fear. (Not even latex anymore!) Stone hot and sweet, eager to please me. Electric skin. Pleased . . .

God, it is wonderful.

April 28, 1995

Stopped over to see Felicia and had a nice conversation with her and Tony, who happened to be there. He pays a lot of attention to her and the girls, as a good uncle. (Because, I think, he's mad at his brother for leaving them.)

Nice to babble on about Stone and how good things are and

feel their warmth and their happiness for me. (So used to the opposite from Uncle Mac, even though he never says it out loud anymore.)

They seem to appreciate the battle Stone's had all his life—all kinds of battles, really, but especially the dyslexia thing. Gave me more credit than I deserve for his renewed ambition. I was surprised to find myself giving some of it to Sonny. I'm still ambivalent about him, grateful for what he's done for Stone, but wishing Stone could, would move on.

Leaving, I heard Tony remark to Felicia how "uncomplicated" young love is. Ha. Doesn't he know that love is better when you get through the complications together? You'd think he would, at his age.

Then I stopped in to see Stone, just to tell him all the nice things they'd said about him. He is amazing, feeling totally rotten physically but extremely optimistic otherwise. (He's having a blood work-up to try to identify this wretched bug and find an antibiotic to wallop the thing.)

Who would have thought a year ago that Stone Cates would be commenting on flowers blooming and the good smell of the spring (and me!) and appreciating life in general? He's actually looking forward to us lying on the grass together this summer and looking up at the clouds.

This, the boy from the streets, who used to be too busy watching his back to look up at all.

The summer stretches like a beautiful green line ahead of us, lazy and happy and loving. I know now that I love Stone with all my heart and that he loves me back, and that whatever the future has for us, that can't change.

May 3, 1995

Joe Scully was killed last night. Shot by Sonny Corinthos. Sonny wasn't held, so it must be true that it was self-defense, but there are a lot of confusing things around it, like the fact that Sonny's father, Mike, was shot, too. May not make it.

What does this mean for Stone? For us? I wish it meant he'd walk away from Sonny, before nobody around him is able to walk. Can't ask Mac any questions. He's going around with that grim "I knew it" look on his face.

Stone, sick as he feels, insists on being available, supportive to Sonny. I have to love him for this, but I am scared and I hate this being scared all the time.

Will this always be a part of loving Stone? The way it was for my mother with Duke? If it is, I will have to live with it. Right now I don't know how.

I want this not to touch us. I want the feeling back that I had the last time I wrote in here. Maybe Tony had a point: love should be simple. But you don't just love somebody when things are perfect.

May 9, 1995
Luke's—waiting

Something worse is wrong, and I don't know what to do.

Stone showed up at the house this morning looking awful and acting like he was in shock. He got as far as saying someone had told him something—obviously something really bad, but then he stopped and wouldn't go on.

I tried to pull the rest out of him, getting more frightened by the minute: was it about Scully and the shooting? Had Mike died? Was Sonny in trouble? Was _he_?

He clammed up. I guess I lost it. I was terrified and I said so: if anything happened to him I don't know what I'd do. Stone turned and ran out of the house!

Mac, God bless him, was not awful about it, but steady and supportive, and to my utter shock said I should go after Stone. I ran—and I found him back at Luke's, but this time he was worse. Snarling. Not him. He said I was crazy, that I couldn't understand English. He told me to go away—not just away but far away and out of his life!

All I could think of was to go see Kevin Collins. Now I'm _sure_ something terrible has happened, because Kevin, who's supposed to be my friend and seems to know, won't tell me.

Patient confidentiality! Like that matters if Stone needs me! How am I supposed to help if I don't know what's wrong? Kevin says Stone loves me—that he's counting on me to love him back— "no matter what." As if I had a choice.

78

I came back here to wait until Stone turned up. Luke and I were both sure he would. But it was Sonny who came through the door. I stared at him and thought, whatever this is, it must have to do with him, because Sonny is the only reason Stone has ever pulled away from me. I looked him in the eye and said so.

Sonny has no clue where Stone is. Faced me down, saying he didn't take him off the street to get him into trouble. It's clear he's worried and covering.

He reminds me we're on the same side.

If that's so, why has Stone run away from us both?

May 10, 1995

Elmwood Park

Where and why would Stone go? Maybe he'll come back here, where Felicia saw him.

Sonny called first thing this morning, trying to be casual but wondering if I'd heard anything. He put forth a theory that Stone, obviously in a "bad mood," maybe went to an all-night movie and fell asleep. Maybe, I said. He's been so tired and can't seem to get rested. We were both whistling in the dark.

Called Jagger in Chicago, trying for casual myself. No word from Stone in several weeks. I said I must have gotten my signals crossed.

The feeling is in two parts that blur over each other: fear and pain. Fear at what's wrong and is he hurt and is he ever coming back, and pain at his shutting me out, and knowing he's hurting and I am powerless.

Mac continues to be incredible. Weird: he has made my life so difficult at times, but when I really, truly need him, he's there, no questions asked. God bless. God keep. (That's Grandma Fil talking.)

I'd almost bought Sonny's all-night movie idea when Felicia turned up at our door, very worried over what was wrong with Stone. She'd seen him here in the park, at dinner time last night, and he was behaving strangely. She tried to speak to him, but he ran from her, too.

I've looked everywhere here that I can think of, all our haunts and special places. If he was here maybe he saw me and ran again. (Ran from me? Stone?)

I went to all the delis and fast food places and showed them the snapshot I carry of him. No one has seen him. They would have to notice him, wouldn't they? Stone is so wonderful looking, you can't just look at him and forget him.

I'm going back to Luke's. I know he won't come to me, but he might, eventually, go to Sonny.

May 12, 1995

Did we live that? Did it really happen? I can't focus, or reconstruct it. Am I dead and in some waiting area of the afterlife? And where, dear God, <u>where</u> is Stone?

Went back to Luke's hoping to see Brenda. Would she know where and why Stone had gone?

Two strange men guarding the place stop me. I'm a friend of Brenda's. They let me pass.

Upstairs, Brenda admits they are extra security, because of Joe Scully. But Joe Scully's dead. I am dense. Why don't I grasp that they're afraid of retaliation? Brenda can't believe it either. Sonny'd told her to leave, but she refused. Sticks by her guy.

One of those guards is dead now. Incredible that Brenda isn't, too. Or me, for that matter. <u>We still don't know about Stone</u>. God, where is he? Please let him be alright. Please bring him back.

We'd worked out a plan, Brenda and I, what to do if Stone didn't show by tomorrow. Meanwhile we would wash our hair and get ourselves together. (Brenda's motto: when feeling helpless, wash your hair.) I headed out, then saw Stone talking to the guards. He froze, and ignored me.

I wouldn't let him. Went to him, begging him to tell me what was wrong, when suddenly there are huge banging sounds and Stone has grabbed me, thrown me down on the ground, thrown himself on top of me.   Glass breaking over us. I realize: the sounds were shots.

Totally still. I try to speak, but Stone covers my mouth, won't let me talk or even move. I'm sure whoever it was is headed back to kill us both, but Stone thinks they've gone up to Sonny's . . . and I remember Brenda's there alone. We start to go to her but—but then see all the blood.

Stone thinks I've been hit, and so do I, frantically searching for a wound. There is none. We realize the wound is his; the blood is his.

I don't know what happened then. I think Stone panicked or something. There was a look of horror on his face—not fear for himself, but some kind of terrible primal dread. He stares, grabs his jacket, and starts frantically to wipe his blood off me, screaming "no, no!" I beg him to stop and help himself—he's the one hurt— but he keeps staring and wiping at the blood on me, desperate. Finally makes a terrible cry like an animal and runs off limping into the dark.

I didn't know what to do. I was numb. Then I remembered Brenda.   I went inside and up to Sonny's apartment. She was there with Harry, shaking in his arms. She'd been in the shower, yes, washing her hair, when a guy burst through the door. She'd sensed something, thrown herself down. When I saw the bullet holes in the shower wall—a line of them in a neat row where her head would have been—I got sick on the spot.

Then Sonny called from Luke's house. They've hit there, too, and two men are dead, but Sonny and Luke and Laura and the chil- dren are okay. Another miracle.

In a daze I called Uncle Mac and he was there in what seemed like one minute, even before the police. Amazingly he didn't say I told you so but just held me while I shook.

The police came. I begged them please to look for Stone, and Uncle Mac took me home.

I can't sleep and I can't think. I want to wake up and find out it didn't happen, that Stone is somewhere near and I can help him. But all I can hear in my head is that animal cry and the sound of his running away.

May 13, 1995
General Hospital, Eighth Floor Solarium

I would have said that yesterday was the worst day of my life, until today.

The police hadn't found Stone this morning, and all I could think about was him hiding somewhere, scared and bleeding. Mac helped. He never said a word against him or threw what had happened in my face. Called the E.R. here to see if they'd had a gunshot wound to report, tried to help me think where Stone might have gone. I racked my brain trying again to think of all the places he might hole up. And suddenly I flashed on the Harborside, the motel where we first made love. And that is where I found him. I told the clerk my "brother" was in trouble and talked him into letting me in the room: Stone is lying on the bed, half out of it, sick and feverish with this bloody, awful bandage he'd tried to put on his leg.

He keeps telling me to go away, he doesn't want me. I say tough, he has me, like it or not, and I don't intend to leave him there to die. I was getting him to the hospital.

He says there's no point; he's going to die anyway. I stare.

Finally he tells me what it was that made him run: Kevin had gotten his blood tests back. He is HIV positive.

It has to be a mistake. That is all I can think of. He'd been tested—Sonny made him do that when he took him off the street, well over three years ago. He was negative then. HIV negative. Stone doesn't understand it either, but he's stopped doubting it. He's positive now.

Most of all he is afraid for me—remembering the times we'd wanted to make love so much we didn't use protection. But that was only a few times. I couldn't have gotten it.

Anyway, how can I think about that now? I have to get him to the hospital.

He didn't want to come here—said he might as well let himself die of the gunshot than go through what he'd have to face. I scrambled for anything halfway positive I'd ever heard, trying not to scream it: HIV doesn't have to mean AIDS. Even if it does, there are people living decent lives, for years. . . . You will. (I will

82

see to it. Dammit, he will.) There's medical help and outreach programs and all kinds of things that he can do. That <u>we</u> can do. And every day more research and more help. They are going to find a solution to this hideous thing and there is no reason to believe they won't find it in time for him.

I couldn't get through. All he seemed to feel was sick and ashamed. And he told me again to go away—get on with my life without him. As if there's any life without . . . oh, God. This is not possible. Not now. Not Stone. Not us.

But I got him here—I had to beg—and Steve Hardy treated his wound. It's superficial but had started to infect. I will love Steve Hardy forever for being so decent and sympathetic and kind as he worked on Stone, so matter-of-fact as Stone cringed with his touch. Not out of pain but fear for anyone who touches him.

Steve assured him he is no danger; they always take precautions. He placed the debris in a waste receptacle labeled "bio-hazard—infectious agent."

Stone read it and said, "Robin, that's me."

Later

Continues, unreal.

At Steve's request, Alan Quartermaine will manage Stone's case. He came in with Kevin, both very shaken. I hope Stone saw this, too. Sounds strange, but I want him to know that other people care. They are not repelled, but concerned. They will help.

Alan took blood for tests, and we are waiting for the results now. They will see if the disease has progressed. But I know it hasn't; it can't have because it hasn't been that long.

Why did Stone test negative and now he isn't?

They explained: it takes six months or so for the virus to produce the antibodies that will show up in the test. So if you've had unprotected sex, you need to be tested again after six months. The first test, just off the street, wasn't enough.

Why didn't Stone know this? Why didn't Sonny? Why didn't I?

How could we not have, with all the AIDS education thrown at us? It's everywhere—schools, books, pamphlets, magazines, all over the media.

Do people, especially young people, just not listen because we don't think it can apply to us? We think AIDS only happens to

83

"certain people"? We tune out and feel superior, or at least totally removed from it?

All the warnings—do they go the way of Don't Smoke, Don't Drink, Don't Get Pregnant? It can't happen to me.

Stone asked me to leave while he told Alan and Kevin how he thought he got it. He's ashamed of the life he led on the street. But I stayed there because I need him to know there is nothing in his past that could make me stop loving him. It is simply a sad story of a lost kid fending for himself out there.

He'd started having sex when he was fourteen, admits he slept around and didn't ask questions, didn't bother with protection. He never used drugs but he had a girlfriend who did. About four years ago. It was around five months after the last time with her that he was tested. He hasn't been with anyone since then—until me.

Kevin explained he should have been tested again. Stone said he wished they'd been around to tell him so.

They say I can go up to the room in a few minutes. Alan requested a private one, so I could stay the night if I want to and Stone wants me to. Like I'd let him stop me. I have to be there when his results come back. They are rushing them through the lab.

Meanwhile I am going to be as positive as I can under the circumstances. I know you can't be "a little HIV" any more than you can be "a little pregnant," but it can't be AIDS yet. It's way too soon.

I didn't want to be tested, because I want to concentrate on Stone right now, but Kevin and Alan made me. I watched my own blood being pulled up into the syringe. It's the same color as Stone's and everyone else's.

May 14, 1995
General Hospital – Stone's room – 2:00 A.M.

It is so still here. All I can hear is Stone's breathing, a little raspy sound at the bottom of each in and out. I put two chairs together next to his bed to make a bed for me, but I can't sleep. Still it is wonderful, being this close to him in the night. I could almost forget, and feeling him so near think it is years from now and we are married and down the hall I could hear the breathing of sleeping children.

84

Every once in a while there is the sound of someone walking by, and now and then the operator pages a doctor, but mostly it is quiet. All I can hear in my head is a jumble of Alan's voice telling us the T-cell count and Kevin talking about being positive and Stone saying it's like Peter Pan: "Think lovelier thoughts, Michael." And I see the faces when it finally got said out loud—Alan's and Kevin's, very solemn, and my own showing whatever numbness looks like.

I'm afraid to write it down because that will make it true. I'm afraid to write it down, but if I don't it will chase me and buzz in my head and will look worse on my face when Stone wakes up. When he wakes up, the first thing I want him to see is the love on my face, not that he has AIDS.

Okay, there it is, what Alan told us the lab test proved: it's not just HIV. Stone has advanced AIDS.

How could it have happened so fast? I've heard of people being HIV positive for years and not getting AIDS.

Alan explains it's a "virulent strain." I see ugly little viruses with teeth, grinning poison and running through his body, a line of them, a "virulent strain," chewing at his immune system. And then (here is your positive thought, Kevin), the medicine, the AZT they're going to start him on right away, going after the viruses, banging at them and crushing them or breathing fire on them, anything to make them disappear.

Stone has AIDS. We know now, Stone has AIDS. But that doesn't mean he's going to die. It doesn't have to mean he's going to die.

May 23, 1995

Last night in the night it seemed true. This morning it doesn't. In the dark and the quiet, somewhere between awake and asleep, it was like this hovering thing that had taken over. I didn't have to think about it. Every cell in my body was absorbing directly the fact that Stone has AIDS. It felt like the truest and the worst thing I'd ever known.

When I woke up there was that feeling you get when you travel and nothing seems usual—the bed feels different under you, the light is coming in from a different angle. You can tell these things before you open your eyes. It took me a few seconds to compute

85

that I wasn't at home. I was in a hospital room. The person next to me whose hand I was holding must be sick—must be Stone. Stone is sick. Stone has AIDS. But that's where I stopped believing—because there was a huge shaft of morning light coming in the window and we were in a hospital, where people get well— and I now think absolutely it was a mistake.

Mistakes get made in laboratories. The people handling the equipment are human. They could mislabel something, or mix up the samples. That happened once in chem lab at school. Somebody got distracted and picked up the wrong test tube and it could have been a disaster but it was averted, I forget how.

Maybe it doesn't happen very often, but it does happen. I've heard stories of doctors even operating on the wrong patient!

Stone is the wrong patient. That has to be true. And some other poor person (I'm sorry) is walking around thinking they're alright.

Later, Elmwood Park

Alan said they'd done the test three times.

He repeated what he'd told us last night. For reference, when I need to convince myself:

The test was a T-cell count. The number of T-cells indicates the level of viral activity in the body. The lower the T-cells, the lower the immune system in your body, and the further the disease has progressed. Normal T-cell count is around 500. Anything under that they begin to question. Anything under 100 is considered very serious.

Stone's T-cell count is 80.

His condition has progressed to advanced AIDS.

It is not a mistake.

The mistake was made four years ago.

They released Stone from the hospital and I went with him back to Sonny's. He's telling Sonny now. I have to go and lie to Mac. I guess it's a good thing I've had so much practice.

Home - 10 P.M.

I got by with a half-truth to Mac: I told him Alan said Stone's wound is healing well. Mac said something about our sitting down and putting things in perspective when I'm ready. It took me a minute to figure out he was talking about the shoot-out at Luke's. I can barely remember it. When was that? Two days ago? And what feels like a whole life. If I try, I can hear the bullets hitting the bricks behind us and feel the glass showering us, but instead of horror I feel a terrible sort of punctuation. New life paragraph: life with AIDS.

Mac is saying something about at my age death seems remote, but he hopes the close call scared me as much as it did him.

I tell him death doesn't seem so remote now.

Later, home

This is the first time I've been alone with myself since we found out. I'm writing things in here compulsively, stupid details: the first thing I did coming home was have a huge dish of peach ice cream. And I remembered feeding Stone ice cream for his monster sore throat that wouldn't go away.

Then I went upstairs and had a conversation with Isabella. I'm not crazy. I've been having conversations with my dolls for years and I saw no reason to stop just because I grew up. (I did, didn't I? I am Robin, all grown up.) There were times (quite a few) when they were the only friends I had. Isabella asked after Stone. She had met him on that blissful "home alone" night. She'd also observed us in my bed. I have no secrets from Isabella.

Isabella, since you ask, Stone isn't well. He's very sick. Sicker than anyone deserves to be. There is this terrible, terrible disease that is killing people, thousands and thousands of people, and it is so bad nobody wants to talk about it. And because nobody wants to talk about it and nobody wants to listen, it's going to kill more.

I want to be optimistic. It's important. It's important for Stone. I will be, I swear it. But the fact is, and I will only say this to you: it is going to kill Stone.

Isabella doesn't say anything back.

She never does. It's one of her best qualities.

Oh, Stone. Oh, Michael. Oh, my love.

Please.

I'm waiting for my test results.   Interesting: in this instance Positive would be Negative. Negative will definitely be Positive. Cute: I'm finding out whether I have a condition that will cause my early death, and what do I do?   Play word games.

I'm scared. I'm scared. I'm scared.

What if I am? What if I have it? What if Stone gave it to me?

If he did, it's not his fault. Or it's as much mine as his. We thought we were safe. We thought his negative test meant we were positively safe.

How could anything as wonderful as making love with Stone make me sick?

I'm really scared.

A little later—in taxi to Stone's

I don't have it. I'm HIV negative. Alan Quartermaine held my hand while he bullied the lab into giving him my results then and there: HIV negative. I know, I know, I have to get tested again in six months. But I won't have it then, either.   Okay, okay, it's still possible. Stone tested negative, too. But at least I can stop thinking about it for six months and think about him.

Later—Stone's Room

Stone cried when I told him. He tried to hide it, but his eyes were wet, and when I put my head on his chest I could feel sobs he didn't want to let out.

He said he could put up with anything they throw at him as long as he knows he didn't hurt me.   I wanted to ask him, "Who are <u>they</u>?" but it didn't seem the time. All I wanted to do was lie there with him and feel his heart beat. And tell him we're in this together and I won't go away.

I won't, Stone. I won't go away. I love you.   I don't think there's any "why" to this or any "they" that did it—unless you count the viruses. I'm with you. You're stuck with me. You didn't hurt me. You could never hurt me. I love you so much.

He reminded me, as gently as he could (Stone is so very, very gentle), that he'd tested negative the first time, too. I promised I'd get retested in six months, but I'm not worried. I won't let myself be. Worry is a waste of time.

There's too much to do in this time. (How much time? How much time? There's no asking and no knowing. No way of measuring it out or planning, except for the most immediate things.)

The wedding. Do we really want to go to a wedding—now? Even of people we love, like Lois and Ned? How can we, with all this awfulness?

But if we don't, aren't we letting the awfulness take over? Maybe if we try, we can go and act as if things are okay. And maybe for that time they could be.

I push, and Stone says yes. A little cynically, but we can work on that.

The problem for me will be travelling and being there with Uncle Mac and not telling him. I wish I could, not because I want to, but because I'd like to get it over with. But Stone isn't ready to go public, and I have to let him deal his way.

At least we won't be alone with the secret. Dr. Quartermaine and Kevin and Steve Hardy will all be there, and of course, Sonny.

Stone had been afraid Sonny would throw him out when he told him about the AIDS, but he was wonderful—supportive, caring, and generous. I'm not really surprised. Sonny Corinthos is a complicated man, but he has a big heart for the people he loves, and he loves Stone. It's the one thing we have in common.

Later—home

Are Sonny and I bonded now? I suppose, in a weird way. All either one wants to do is the best thing for Stone.

So far we agree on the obvious—see he takes care of himself, takes the medication, try to keep a positive attitude. Positive attitude. Positive attitude.

Also, Kevin told Sonny we should encourage Stone to tell people as soon as he can—at least the ones he trusts—because the burden of the secret can cause stress which his immune system definitely doesn't need.

Sonny Corinthos went to see a psychiatrist? The mind boggles. He said Stone had suggested it. Stone probably meant it to help Sonny, and Sonny did it to help Stone, but whatever. I'm touched that he'd go that far for him.

Farther, really. Stone told me Sonny matter-of-factly offered to pay all his medical expenses.   God bless, God keep, Sonny. And God keep me from thinking about where that money is coming from.

May 29, 1995
Oyster Bay, New York
The Wedding

Imagine having a whole huge house you save just for special occasions. With enough rooms to put up a hoard of wedding guests plus your own big family. Of course they wouldn't need to use so many rooms if the people who are sleeping together (the unmarried ones) were rooming together, but there is a lot of propriety going on here, I guess for Mrs. Quartermaine's sake.

Wouldn't it be funny if everyone got the same idea at the same time and we all met each other tiptoeing down the hall in the middle of the night? Like Grand Central Station, but everybody in bathrobes: Jason and Keesha, Sonny and Brenda (although I doubt they would since they had a big fight on the train down), Simone and Justus, me and Stone. . . . I wonder what Lila Quartermaine would think of me if she knew Stone and I are sleeping together. Were.

Actually, I think Lila Quartermaine, in spite of her Grande Dame look, is a pretty liberal lady, and she'd probably think I was pretty lucky. Was. (Dammit, I have to stop whining about it. My sex life is the least of things.)

"Wedding Train" down

Tense fun. Ned and Lois manic, try to get everyone as happy as they are. Tough order, with Brenda looking daggers at Sonny and Lily (who are, I really think, just friends) and Miguel sulking and Sonny brooding. And Audrey Hardy glaring at Justus Ward because Simone is still legally her daughter-in-law, etc.

But bride-and-groom state-of-mind takes over and a crazy, joyful conga line weaves around the tables, past Lila Quartermaine sitting in her wheelchair like a challenged queen, around Stone and me, hugging each other and keeping the rhythm (as best Stone can with his bad leg). For a while it works the way I hoped it would: we have fun, and for some of the time, manage to forget and just Be There.

Need to make this keep happening.   It will take a lot of planning and maneuvering, but I will. We will have wonderful, beautiful times together. I will show him and tell him everything I can, and I will listen to everything he ever wanted to say, until we can't any more.

May 30, 1995,

Oyster Bay
Rehearsal Party on the "Lila"

Brenda and Sonny made up and the yacht almost sank. (Not necessarily cause and effect there; just what happened.)

Turned out Brenda had been angry that Sonny wouldn't share something big that was troubling him. (She thought he'd told Lily, but he hadn't.) This was, of course, Stone's illness, because Stone had asked him not to.   Soon as Stone found out he said please go ahead and tell her (good; it's a first step for him to going public), but Sonny said he'd wait until after the wedding. He and Brenda went up on deck, and I guess he told her he'd tell her, because they were all cuddly and snuggly afterward. I'm glad for Lois and Ned (and the rest of us) because all that glowering was sure casting a pall on the party.

The almost shipwreck (boatwreck? yachtwreck?) seems almost slapstick now (all those dressed-up people baling seawater in the bilge, Lois's twin nephews running around shouting "We're sinking, we're sinking,") but there was a moment when I was terrified Stone and I were going to lose each other and not even have whatever time we have.

I hate to say it (and I wouldn't anywhere else), but I think it happened because of Edward Q's need to show off to the Cerullos. (You would think being tried for murder would have given him a little humility, but I guess not.) He insisted the Captain move in closer to land to give everyone a better view of the lights of Coney Island.

91

The Captain warned him about the rocks, but Mr. Q. was flaunting his authority, and pretty soon there was this sickening crunch and "The Lila" had been holed.

I wish Stone and I could have been on the bucket brigade, only because he felt useless. The worst moment for me wasn't getting on the life jackets and singing "Nearer My God to Thee" (yes, we actually did), it was Stone saying drowning would solve a lot of problems.

I'm so confused. How is he supposed to stay positive but also express his feelings, when sometimes they're just the opposite?

Mine, too, but I'm working on it. And if I act positive all the time, am I being honest with Stone? Up to now honesty has been the basis of our relationship (give or take a few areas we know better than to discuss).

Maybe I'll try to talk to Kevin about this. He's more than willing to help. I wish I believed he could. Stop it, dammit. Up, up, UP!

Okay. Here's something useful I learned from the experience: Stone can't swim. I will teach him this summer (if I can get my city boy in the water). Yes, I will. How's that for positive?

June 1, 1995
"Wedding Train" back

Stone nauseous this whole trip back. Our story: reaction to pain medication he got for his leg. He's dozing now and I'm trying to cover him so nobody notices. I'm not really large enough to do that, but everyone's involved in their own conversations, mostly about the wedding—how beautiful Lois looked, how happy she and Ned were—so he isn't attracting any attention.

Is that how it's going to be from now on? Covering for Stone? And when he finally gets brave enough to tell people he's got AIDS, what will my role be then? Buffer their reactions? Educate them about the virus? —That they shouldn't be afraid of him, but they should be afraid of it, and protect themselves in their lives? Support him, hold his hand, see he doesn't isolate, see he follows his regimen, try to raise his spirits? I think I know how the people in the bilge felt when they were trying to bale.

I don't know if I'm large enough.

All right, sufficient venting. "Think lovelier thoughts." Wedding. Lois in Lila's gown. Vibrant. Joyful. She and Ned breathless with happiness. They earned it.

Brenda, Best Person, looking so pleased with herself for having gotten them together. Umpteen bridesmaids, all related to Lois (except for Emily, a last-minute addition, looking ten-year-old earnest and careful coming down the aisle).

Church filled: cousins, aunts, uncles, grandparents, Quartermaines, and friends. How can one person have so many relatives? Strange how these are distributed. I am related by blood to only one alive person on earth: Mac Scorpio. There are other ways to be related, though.

Till death do us part.

Stone stirs a little, turns his head. I think how long his hair has grown since I first knew him, since we stood together, Best People, as Karen and Jagger took the same vows Ned and Lois did this morning.

I remember how when we were first friends—casual friends (Ha. Never.)—I used to want to reach out and touch his hair. It always looked so silky. I reach out and touch it now. I have the right, publicly. I want people to see how much I love him. (But they're still talking about the wedding and don't notice us.)

Midnight—home

I meant it, Stone. Every word of it, with every cell of me:

I, Robin Scorpio, make this vow to you, Michael Cates. I promise to stay by your side and never leave you. I vow to give you the happiest days of both our lives for as long as you will let me. I will protect you and defend you against anyone who might hurt you. I will love and cherish you, honor and respect you, for richer and for poorer, through sickness and in health . . .

I had to stop there. I couldn't seem to say the rest. Stone finished it for me:

Till death do us part.

An hour ago, downstairs, in the living room, wearing my mother's mantilla. I'd only meant to show it to him, tell him about my

93

little girl fantasy of wearing it to my own wedding. The wedding had made him thoughtful about serious things he'd never considered—how it would be to stand front of people who care and make vows that mean you have a chance of growing old together.

He took the mantilla and put it over my hair, so gently I could barely feel it, and said I would be an amazing bride. He wished he could be there. I said maybe . . . but he stopped me and said to be realistic. So I was. I took his hands and promised those things and meant them. All I asked him to promise was that he'll never, ever try to push me away.

Lois & Ned
May 31 1995

Lois & Ned May 31 1995

CLOSE COVER •• STRIKE ON BACK

June 5, 1995

I am amazed by the dailiness of things, still. At school I turn in my term papers and my lab reports and get ready for finals. I talk prom plans with my friends. I make notes for my valedictory speech, barely noticing the irony of "onward and upward" rhetoric. I receive preliminary reading lists from Yale for my selected cours-es. I get the books from the library. (I don't open them.) Priorities seem to sort themselves out unconsciously.

Stone and me.

June 6, 1995

One more person to help: Sonny told Brenda, and she's as fierce about this as anyone else who loves Stone. Loves Us. In a weird way seeing someone else feel terrible about this helps. Not that I want anyone hurting, but this is so beyond terrible I need to see it reflected in someone else's face—not just the pain, but the anger.

It's hard to let the anger happen because it's so overwhelming I'm afraid to let it out—I'm sure it will turn around and swallow me. Or consume me from the inside out. I guess anything you don't let yourself feel will do that, but it's so exhausting, _feeling_ all the time. Everything.

Stone thought he should see Brenda right away after Sonny told her. I wish I could have been with him for that, but as much as I want to, I can't hold his hand through everything. He needs to know he's strong enough to face things, to face people by himself.

When Brenda moved to hug him, she said his whole body was stiff, I suppose with fear and defense. But she wouldn't give up, just kept hugging, and finally she felt him give in and let her love him. What broke her heart was the shame on his face. (We will erase it, all of us, together, we _will_.)

That is the worst, the absolutely cruelest part of this disease. It's not enough that the virus attacks everything in you that can fight physically. (Clever virus. So effectively indirect.) It attacks what you think of yourself, by the way people react to you. Or the way you think they will.

I truly know that all the people who love Stone (so many more than he knows) will support him, will be everything they can to

96

him. That the horror he'll inevitably see on their faces when they find out will be <u>for</u> him, not <u>at</u> him.

But I know that Stone is right, too. There will be others who show disgust and fear and rejection. What they'll really be showing is stupidity and shallowness, but that's not going to help much when it hits.

He's afraid the world will wonder how he got it. Of course they will. It's everyone's first question, even if they don't say so. It was mine, wasn't it? Was I accusing him by asking? I don't think so. I just needed to know. Actually, I suppose it's a question people have to ask if they're to get educated. Answer: Stone got AIDS by having indiscriminate sex. You could, too.

June 8, 1995

I see I avoided the obvious above: so could I. If you call sex without a condom indiscriminate, and I guess that's fair.

I don't want to dwell on it. I told Brenda, when I couldn't reassure her that we'd used protection: I absolutely will not spend the whole summer and fall until I get tested again worrying about whether I'm HIV positive. Stone needs me too much, and our time together is too precious.

She said that was either the most loving, unselfish thing she'd ever heard, or I was in so much denial it scared her to death.

Scared to death. Just the opposite, wasn't it? Fearless to death. Careless to death. Stupid to death. Dammit, I wasn't going to dwell on it. If I can't "think lovelier thoughts," I'd better try not to think at all. Very funny. I'm me, remember? Thinking R Us.

June 10, 1995
Wyndham's Coffee Bar

Here's something much better to obsess about: I can't find a prom dress. Everything I try on makes me look either like Little Miss Muffet or a Front Street hooker.

Then there is the heavy question of accessories. I would like to carry my mother's French brocade evening bag, but it does limit the kind of dress I get. Can't be too elaborate because the bag is pretty busy. Well, elaborate's not great on me anyway. I am too small and wind up getting lost in it.

Should I do short or long? Long is more elegant, but harder to dance in. But short . . . well the buzz is that girls who wear those really short dresses are planning to "lose it" that night. Makes sense in terms of efficiency, I guess, but seems a little calculated. (Robin, excuse me, but do you or do you not remember changing your underwear three times while dressing for the evening of February 4?) Anyway, at least I don't have to worry about looking virginal anymore.

They are going to flip when they meet him. It seems strange I never took him to a school social function before this, but it never felt appropriate, or I thought he would be bored or something. He seems so beyond all those kids.

I sincerely hope everyone realizes I'm sleeping with Stone. I'd like to pin a sign to the back of his tux. (Okay, so it's not true right now. As I told Brenda, I simply won't entertain the idea of never making love with him again. We will figure out something.)

June 11, 1995

I've got to stop censoring Stone. I didn't even realize I was, until Brenda told me he'd been able to let out some anger to her and I had this pang of jealousy that made me ashamed.

But when Stone gets cynical or makes black-humor jokes, I get crazy. What do I think—if we never refer to the fact that death is lurking, it will get discouraged and go away?

Like today when I went over to see him and bring him my happy news about the San Francisco cohort—this group of guys who contracted HIV fifteen years ago and are still alive—and he didn't get excited, I felt, I don't know, rejected or reprimanded or something.

Actually all he was doing was feeling what he felt, and I was the one who was rejecting that. Feeling obliged to get in there and correct it. He said something about having one foot in the grave, and I got mad, so he said, "Excuse me, think positive, there's one foot out of the grave."

It's not just that it scares me to hear him say those things, it makes me <u>mad</u>, because I can't stand the thought of giving in to this virus without the biggest, strongest, noisiest fight we can put up. And grasping at every shred of hope is part of that fight.

I said that, and I guess I must have reached him, because he stared at me and asked where I'd come from and if I know how much he loves me. Genuine wonder.

And I thought, a moment like that—people could live years and not have a moment that beautiful. It is the strangest sort of blessing. I only hope he knows it goes both ways.

Somehow that connection made it possible for me not to cringe when he said he'd been thinking about death. What it's like, what happens. He stopped, afraid he was bumming me out, but I said no, I wanted to hear, and for the first time, I did.

He wondered if you just evaporate, like you were never here. Or if it was like going to sleep, and if it was, did you dream. He said if that's what it is, like sleeping in my arms, and dreaming about me . . . maybe it wouldn't be so bad.

I hope it is gentle and beautiful and peaceful and that there is some kind of joy. Somehow I feel there has to be.

But I can't help thinking what it will be like to miss him in my arms, dream about him, and still be alive.

June 12, 1995

Further Heavy Prom Problem: Shoes. My dilemma: do I opt for comfort or looks? (I.e., flats or heels?)

Flats would feel better, but would require me to spend the evening staring at the third button on Stone's shirt. Also they wouldn't look so great with the dress. Heels would, if you don't count the limp they'll give me by the middle of the evening.

Brenda—help! Panic rises. Not only don't I have shoes, but I hate the dress that Wyndham's is holding. What possessed me to choose empire crushed velvet with pouffe sleeves? What do I think this is, "War and Peace?"

Brenda soothes me, reassures me, tells me there is a pair of shoes out there. Also that Prom Anxiety is a well-documented condition, curable only by doing what you fear: actually dressing up and going. Quite normal, Brenda says, and she ought to know. <u>Why</u>, come to think of it? Brenda's life has been anything but. Who wants normal anyway? I gave it up, remember?

The truth is, I don't think shoes are what's scaring me. It's taking Stone into a group of regular teenagers who are busy planning their futures. It seems like a cruel thing to do. Not only that, maybe he doesn't have the stamina yet and he'll be pushing himself for my sake. I don't want that. No dumb dance is worth his feeling any worse.

Later

We're going, and that's that. My love has spoken. He wants to go with me, give me a corsage, dance every dance, make the other guys jealous, drink awful punch with me, the whole number. He will not be cheated of these major life experiences, he insists. He wants to see me in my dress.

Omigod, my dress.

I hate my dress.

June 13, 1995

All is well. I found another one. When I went to Wyndham's to pick up the one I really didn't like, they'd gotten in a whole new shipment—probably in preparation for the Nurses' Ball. It is blue, royal blue, in soft embossed silk, long, simple, form-fitting but not clingy, and I feel vaguely regal in it. (If anyone 5'1" can be regal.) Even a little sexy. I really, really love it and I really, really want to go and hold my guy dancing and show the world how much in love we are. No matter what.

Oh, and I found shoes, too. Now the burning question is whether to wear my hair up or down.

June 15, 1995

3 P.M.

Uncle Mac's more pumped about our after-prom breakfast than I am. Seems to have some profound, avuncular meaning to him. Sweet, really.

He first brought this up when we were sitting waiting for Lois to arrive at her wedding. At the time I thought he was trying to distract me from the fact that I was sitting in a church with Stone. At a wedding, with Stone. And that he came up with this idea for a prom breakfast at the Outback to distract me from what that might call to mind (a future together).

How self-centered and paranoid can you get? That was so rotten of me, when all he was trying to do was make me happy.

So there he is this morning planning the logistics of the whole thing and the breakfast menu and swearing his adult supervision would be undetectable (ha). It is dear of him to do this. At least I had the sense to tell him so.

I also felt bad that I kind of overdid the romance thing to Miguel, babbling about the prom. I had no idea that he and Lily had split up. She gave him back his engagement ring.

Is she crazy? If I didn't think they were in love it would be different, but you can tell by the way they look at each other, even when they're angry (especially when they're angry), that they are. How can she be such a fool, to give up and walk away when they could be together?

I want to shake her and say, "Don't be stupid! Treasure the time you have together, don't trash it!"

Later

Stone came over to the Outback at noon and is looking and feeling better, which makes me less nervous about tonight.

Oh, yes, I also got a job today. I wasn't looking for one, but I got one. A.J. and Jason and Keesha recruited me to work at the Charles Street Foundation. I said no at first, that I had "other plans," meaning Stone, but they caught on and assured me I'd have "plenty of time" for Stone. (They don't know, of course, that he's sick.) Like there's plenty of time for anything.

But Stone encouraged me to take the offer. It's important to him that I don't let his illness take over my life. So I won't, for his sake.

—Is that vaguely contradictory? I don't care. I accepted, and I think it will be fun and satisfying working for a worthy operation. Also, making some money that is not paid to me by my uncle, for a change.

It is time to stop procrastinating and begin the Ritual. That which has been performed by millions of other young women before me. There are only four hours left. I have to start to Get Ready for The Prom. (Bring up chorus. And maybe some bells.)

June 16, 1995

I will not allow the behavior of one bigoted pig to be my main memory of prom night. I will remember everything wonderful first, then include the awful part as a footnote, which is all it deserves. It is Stone who taught me that. Amazing.

Pre-prom: Makeup and hair attended to (went for Up because Stone's never seen it that way), I am still in my bathrobe trying on every pair of earrings I own, when Brenda arrives to offer moral support and a sweet gift: an elegant silver bracelet she's had engraved: "To My Little Sister." To remind me she loves me and I can count on her. I would have cried, but she wouldn't let me, afraid for my mascara.   She hugs me and then points me directly to the right earrings.

Then Felicia comes up (she and Maxie have come to Observe), and when Brenda leaves, she switches into Mother mode. I don't mind this; in fact, it's very nice. I have a flash of how it might have been, Anna Scorpio up here in my room, fussing over me and trying not to cry. My father downstairs with the camera ready.

When I snap back Felicia is saying things I identify as trying to "draw me out." Seems Mac has expressed some concern. (He probably put her up to this.) Something doesn't seem right, since the shooting at Luke's. Are things okay with Stone?

I tell her the one thing I am absolutely sure of is loving Stone. Sometimes so much it hurts. She says she can relate.

More hugs; Felicia goes. I get into my dress, stare at myself in the mirror. My figure is better than it used to be. The shape of my face seems more definite. There is something more in my eyes— not my mother's fire, but something else that is mine. I suspect that all of this, I'm not sure how, has to do with Stone. I hope he likes the way I look. God knows I tried.

The doorbell rings downstairs. I don't move. No girl should be this ready for her escort.

The prom is everything it should be—romantic, intense, a little unreal.   My girlfriends drool over Stone; their guys are impressed and annoyed about it.

Vivid sense memory: Stone and me clinging to each other, barely moving, calling it dancing—a sort of dreamlike sway to "I'll Stand By You."   It's like we have melted together and everything beautiful and terrible has melted together with us. This is another moment I will always have. I push away the feeling of collecting them and manage to be there.

The next sense is of Stone's hands on my face, outside the Outback, trying to keep me from shaking with rage, calming me with his eyes. Saying it's bad enough AIDS is cheating us out of our future. If we let it take away the present, then we're just letting it win. This seems familiar, and I realize it sounds like me.

He's right, but I'd do it again: throw Kirk Miller out of my party for his vile stupid disgusting cruel AIDS jokes. Stone says he has to get used to this. It's part of the disease. The sick people who laugh at other people's pain. I suppose the scene I made will become a piece of prom lore, class of '95. And Stone's probably right: you can't change people.

But some things you have to fight about. Some things have to be yelled. If we don't do this, AIDS will kill all of us, one way or another.

Stone's boutonniere

Freesia from my corsage

OUTBACK

BREAKFAST

**Mac Scorpio cordially invites you
to a midnight breakfast**

at the

OUTBACK

Following the

"Port Charles High School Senior Prom"

June 18, 1995

Graduation

An enormous tent has been set up on the lawn of Port Charles High School. Large enough for a circus. The graduates waiting in line are sweltering under nylon gowns that don't breathe—gold for girls, royal blue for boys—and feeling various degrees of ridiculous under medieval headgear. It rained at eleven, so the grass around the tent is still wet, dampening everybody's summer shoes. It feels like steam is rising from the ground.

Trumpet Voluntary. Everyone comes to attention, stands. The band begins "Pomp and Circumstance," which it will play over and

106

over and over (it is a large class). The graduates parade in two by two, expressions from solemn to vapid to embarrassed to scared. A carefully unreligious convocation is delivered, followed by greetings from more officials than anyone knew were involved. The class valedictorian rises to make her speech. She is short, dark-haired, poised, well-spoken, and feeling disembodied.

She is aware of a voice, apparently hers, delivering a speech she apparently wrote, and aware of her personal supporters, watching pridefully from the third row: uncle, surrogate mother and little sister, surrogate big sister, love of her life. She finishes to substantial applause and the five of them stand, followed by the rest of the audience. The love of her life lets out a street-sounding whistle.

More speeches, appropriate medley by the chorus, awards, presentation of diplomas. She is grateful that from her prominent position on stage she won't have far to walk. She has a long wait, her surname being far down in the alphabet. One by one her classmates walk past her as their names are intoned and collect their diplomas. Some are confident, some are nervous, some are arrogant.

In a major contribution to graduation lore, a blond jock named Kirk Miller trips on his way across and hits the stage with his knees, in front of his parents and everybody. God is good.

Port Charles High School
Class of 1995
Commencement June 18th 1995

Congratulations on this your Graduation day
May Happiness and Success Be Yours Always

June 19, 1995

Stone's T-cells are up! His T-cells are up! 80 to 120! He finds me outside the Outback, picks me up, spins me around, practically tosses me in the air. I want to yell with joy, but he stops me. Mac's inside, might wonder.

Mac ran into him at the hospital, gave him a ride home (!), Stone manufacturing cover story all the way. Still, it is progress. Until Mac finds out why he was at the hospital, and why we have reason to rejoice, temporarily; why we are counting T- cells.

June 27, 1995

Barely have a chance to catch our breath from graduation, and we are into the Nurses' Ball.

Stone and I went over this morning to help Lucy and Jon Hanley set up. This was the price I had to pay to get Lucy to stop hounding us to do another scene from Shakespeare this year. She insisted our "Romeo and Juliet" was the hit of the evening (yeah, like with Uncle Mac) and wouldn't we please, please, please . . . but I pointed out to her that a death scene is a hard act to follow.

What blew us away were the panels from the AIDS quilt. Jon had managed to acquire several large segments for display at the ball, and explained the Names Project to us. I knew a little about it, but no one could prepare you for the effect when you see even a portion of a quilt that now numbers about 28,000 handmade panels, each commemorating a person who died from complications of AIDS. And that number represents only a small proportion of the people who've actually been affected.

Jon Hanley is a fantastic example for Stone. Diagnosed <u>nine years ago</u>, and is going strong. He says ironically he's in the best shape he's ever been. He takes care of himself and does everything the doctors tell him and keeps his attitude where it should be. Stone wondered that he never gets angry. Jon said yes he does, but it depends what he does with it.

Jon's also very open about his condition, good for Stone to see. I know the secret is draining him and he needs that energy.

Truthfully, it's draining me, too. The idea of being at the ball tonight—a ball to benefit AIDS programs at GH—and acting as though everything is fine doesn't make sense.

But it's not my call. Stone will do it when he's ready.

Midnight, afterwards

I didn't have to wait very long. I know Stone didn't mean for it to happen tonight or the way it came out, but maybe God did. In any case, Stone's AIDS is no longer a secret, and I'm waiting up for Uncle Mac to be sure he hears it from me and no one else.

The evening was weird to start with. Being there with most of Port Charles society all done up in their fanciest (there were some incredible dresses, most of which were worn by Lucy Coe), watching a lot of people I know in other capacities sing and dance and act silly, to benefit a disease the man sitting beside me has. All the talk about it—Ryan White's mother (God, what must it be like to lose a child to this?), the quilt pieces, Jon Hanley's incredible, painful speech about AIDS prejudice all brought it home—probably closer than anyone there wanted. One thing consistent about AIDS is the way it makes everyone acutely uncomfortable. The well-meaning try to deal but would rather do it at a distance.

I saw Stone move over and speak to Jon afterwards. I think he was saying thank you. Then he came back to the table where we were sitting with assorted Quartermaines.

Jason, of course, was with Keesha, and A.J. seemed to be showing off Lily Rivera as his date, rubbing it in by inviting Miguel to join us at the table. Miguel was very cool and polite and sat down with us. Whereupon A.J. went into complete jackass mode and started spouting this stuff about AIDS—how Jon was right, that it should be treated like any other disease.

At first we were all stunned that he'd voiced a liberal opinion, but he went on to say other diseases needed money and attention, too, and why should AIDS get it all?

Stone was sitting very close to me and I felt him begin to tremble. He called A.J. on his point of view, saying if we didn't solve it, AIDS could kill all of us. A.J. scoffed, as only A.J. can, and retorted that nobody but gays and people so stupid they deserved it let themselves get exposed to AIDS.

Stone was shaking now as he cited Ryan White and all the others—were they stupid? Did they deserve it? Everybody was silent, appalled, but A.J. kept at it, then stopped abruptly, wondering out loud when Stone became such an expert on AIDS?

Stone said when he found out he had it.

Thick silence and stunned faces. Even Alan's, who knew, but

hardly expected it to come out this way. A.J. sputters, stammers, attempts to say I'm sorry. Stone says, "So what?" and we leave the table. He goes to tell Lois and Ned right away so they don't hear it anywhere else.

When he comes back we sit with Brenda and Sonny at their table as Miguel goes on to sing. He speaks to the audience quietly, clearly in pain, saying he'd just learned a friend of his has AIDS. It made him realize, he says, how desperately we need to find a cure. Then he sings "The Power to Believe" and dedicates it to his friend, whose hand I am holding beside me.

It's hardly the way I would have chosen it to come out—but what way would have been good—what way would make people comfortable—and why should they be? I'm glad it happened. It is a major relief, and now at least we have a different kind of fear.

RAINBOW OF HOPE

The Second Annual
General Hospital Nurses' Ball

To Benefit
The Combined AIDS - Related Programs
at General Hospital

June 28, 1995, 3 A.M.

What did I think? That I would say, "Uncle Mac, Stone has AIDS," and he'd say, "Gosh, honey that's a pity"?

How would I have planned it, to make it better? Tell him some "kinder, gentler" way?

I knew he would be angry. I knew he would be appalled at our being irresponsible (even though we thought we weren't). I wasn't even surprised (though it stung) when he said, "Robin, how could you be that stupid?" Because this is a question I ask myself, when I can't shut it out.

I knew he would be frightened, though it would take him time to admit it, and when he did, he would hold me, which he did, finally.

But I didn't know, I never thought he could, have no compassion at all for Stone.

Uncle Mac, you have truly failed me. Not because you failed to protect me, which is what I know you think, but because you can't share my pain, and I need to share it. More than that, Stone needs all of us. He is so, so sick.

No, this is wrong, not fair: I'm doing to you what I find myself doing to Stone—not letting you have your feelings. It's immediate anger, but you'll get over it and feel for him. Your heart is too big not to. You haven't failed me—yet.

I went down the hall just now, looking for you (hoping we could just sit together awhile), but you weren't there. I wonder if you're out somewhere, walking and hating Stone.

I know you love me and you're scared. But hating Stone now is the worst thing you could do to me. You can't know how alone it makes me feel.

I know you need to blame, but if you do, you have to blame us both—Stone and me. We both made choices, we both were naive, we both made love because we both wanted to. Please don't go away from me now. I need you.

Same, around 10:00 P.M.

It's weird how people react to horrible, threatening things. Uncle Mac made pancakes.

I suppose this is some kind of control gesture.

Only he couldn't. He got mixed up and started to stir the batter in the pan, thinking for the moment it was eggs. The result was funny, which we needed.

Actually I know it wasn't so much control as love. Making breakfast for me was the only thing he could think of to do. It said all kinds of things, but it didn't say he felt any different about Stone.

He told me where he was last night: Felicia's, trying to blame her because she'd recommended I get on the pill. God, how that must have hurt her. To find out that way and face his rage, too.

I told him no way was it her fault, but he had already figured that out, and told her, too. He admitted he was looking for someone else to blame because <u>he</u> felt responsible. I tried hard to tell him he wasn't, but I don't think I got through. He feels he betrayed the trust of his brother, and that's enormous for him.

I'm going over to see Felicia. I hope she understands why I didn't tell her sooner.

Later

She did, of course. And she tried to be as supportive and calm as possible, but I could see the fear in her for me. I tell her no way is she responsible, and I think she understands that in her head, but I can see somewhere she blames herself.

I try hard to reassure her: I'm alright. I can't let myself be scared. Stone is who we have to think about. Focus on him—on making his life as good as we can. That's what love is. She can't seem to speak, just hugs me, but it's clear she agrees.

Clear too, though, that she's still afraid. It's really awful to watch people you love blame themselves.

Later

You know who was especially wonderful? Luke Spencer. Not just to Stone, but to me. He's keeping him on the job, which amazed Stone, but is not so surprising. He was Daddy's best friend, and Daddy knew how to pick people. When Luke said, "Stuff happens. It's nobody's fault, and nobody's to blame," it was almost like I was hearing my father's voice. Maybe I was.

And here is something really wild: who turns up at Sonny's door this afternoon but Jason Quartermaine? He's aware it's important for people in Stone's condition to keep fit with regular exercise. As it happens, he needs a workout partner. Offers Stone to come and use the Quartermaine state-of-the-art fitness room, on a regular basis, starting today.

I have always known Jason to be one of the best people on God's earth.

June 29, 1995

How can I keep Stone safe from stupidity? From the cruelty that comes out of cowardice?

The kindest thing I can say about A.J. Quartermaine at the moment is he is insecure and damaged in some way. Ignorant, and noisy about it. Puffed up, pathetic, to be pitied rather than despised. And I still want to wring his neck.

Jason had arranged a picnic for us after Stone's first work-out with him, and though I felt self-conscious, like everyone would be trying too hard for us, it turned out to be quite hilarious and fun.

Brenda and Miguel, in an attempt to practice their video dance routine on the lake wall, tripped and fell in, and there was a lot of laughter and good feeling (although not, I'd have to say, from Sonny). But I thought I saw something behind Stone's eyes, and later he told me what had happened at the work-out:

He was spotting weights for A.J., who of course was showing off as usual, and looked like he was going to drop one. Stone leaned forward over him and some sweat dropped from him onto A.J. A.J. dumped the weight fast and lunged away, frantically wiping himself with a towel. There was a big ugly silence and Jason said ("very quiet and classy"—per Stone), "You don't get AIDS from sweat, A.J."

How, please, how can I spare him this kind of humiliation, this kind of pain? This is exactly what he feared the most—people acting like he's dirty, and making him feel he really is.

I tried the one way I could think of to counter it: when we went back to his room, I asked him to make love to me. (This was hardly a selfless idea; I really wanted to. Oh, did I.) I said of course we'd use protection, it would be fine, I couldn't stand to lose that part of our life.

He took my arms from around him and backed away. <u>Stone backed away from me.</u> Just looked at me and said, "Robin, it's out of the question. How can you ask me to put you in danger?"

So I ended up making him (and me) feel worse.

There has to be a way that's safe.

July 3, 1995

How can I keep on forgiving Uncle Mac when he keeps on making things even worse?

Mac told me himself (not wanting me to hear it elsewhere) that he'd run into Stone and tried not to say anything beyond hello. He was afraid he couldn't control himself, which turned out to be true.

The awful thing is, Stone seems to have wanted Mac to go off on him. Figuring I guess it would help Mac (and me) if he could vent his anger in the right direction. (Except Stone isn't the right direction. The Universe, or whatever, is.) But he gave Mac the opening, and Mac let him have it between the eyes. Lethal, horrible thrust: something to the effect that Stone may have signed my death warrant!

I'm not going to ask how could he. I've asked that too many times about too many lesser things. I'm not even angry. I told him I'm beyond angry.

This is new information for me: that Uncle Mac could be that cruel under the lame excuse of loving me.

A horrifying side-effect of AIDS: showing us other people at their worst—their smallness, meanness, cruelty. The casualty is our fantasy of what we thought they were—and the shock and disappointment of what they aren't.

Everything, all this time, was supposed to be because Mac loves me. I don't buy it. I think all this time he just needed to be right. And I told him so.

Fourth of July, 1995

It's like the old days at home, Mac and I barely acknowledging each other. I made our own picnic and Stone and I went to the park with everyone else, but we kept to ourselves.

Stone says he understands Mac's position perfectly and wishes I could, because I'm going to need Mac . . . he starts to say "after" but I won't let him.

What he doesn't understand is why I'm not mad at him the way Mac is, because he believes what Mac said—he may have given "it" to me. It almost scares him that I don't feel angry. He wonders why.

117

I don't really know. Maybe, I tell him, because he means more to me than anything in the world.

The smell of summer, low voices reading the Declaration of Independence (copies courtesy of the city council), bursts of light, color, loud sound. Mary Mae singing "America the Beautiful," a capella, straight from the gut. Families on blankets with kids. I suppose as a "people" we are independent, but as persons, individually, is anybody? Does anybody really want to be?

July 5, 1995

Today I poured coffee and gave out press kits as we officially announced the federal matching grant A.J. managed to get for the Charles Street Foundation. (No small accomplishment in today's political climate.) He also introduced the first recipient of a small business loan. (A nice plumber; that part made me feel good.)

Actually, I wanted to quit CSF after the ugly sweat thing with A.J., but Stone wouldn't let me. He says one of the things AIDS is teaching him is tolerance—needing acceptance makes him realize he has to give it, too: "Nobody's all black or white, Robin."

Who knew Stone Cates would wind up more liberal than me?

I have to admit (grudgingly) that A.J. seems to be doing a good job. Too bad he's so aware of it himself. There he was strutting around, Mr. Glad-hand with the press, showing off mostly for his grandfather's benefit, I think, but also sticking it to Ned, whom he's never gotten along with.

Don't you love it?—I Invoke Tolerance, then diss A.J. for a paragraph. Well, sometimes you've got to diss somebody or something. The Universe is just too general.

July 7, 1995

Things are going on around me, but I just don't seem to connect to them. A few days after our triumph, now there's a mess at the Foundation, due apparently to A.J.'s grant application making it look like the CSF is just a Quartermaine tax dodge. It's not that I don't care—I'm sorry about it, I'm sure it will blow over, and I just can't find any mind space to keep it in.

Stone worries that his illness is the focus of my life. He's wrong. He is the focus of my life. I'm sure it would be the same if he were well.

My mind takes off there a minute, wondering how it would be, what we would be doing, if he were well. Not so much different, I think (except we would be making love a lot). We'd still be spending all the time we could together, but we wouldn't know how precious it is.

Would I have gotten used to him? I mean, to us? Would I still be getting that dazed feeling in my stomach when I look at his eyebrows or his jawline, his smile, which is sweeter and sweeter to me?

He has always had this look of wonderful amusement in his eyes. Early on it was more cynical, but now it's more appreciative (if sometimes ironic). He is funnier, it seems to me, than he used to be. Pretty strange, under the circumstances, but maybe this is another one of God's backward gifts. Like loving each other more every day. Maybe even more than we would have.

July 9, 1995

We are coming up, in a few weeks, to the anniversary of the Night of the Bear. I told Stone I wanted to plan a hike and a picnic (maybe just on the edge of the game reserve?) to celebrate, but he said, "What's to celebrate?" That hurt so much, but I didn't want to let him see it, because he's already struggling with so much guilt over me.

I see that whole incident—the hike, the bikers and the bear— as a major turning point in our relationship. After all, it was when Mac gave up on trying to stop us. And after that, we had that incredible summer. When I point this out, Stone finally smiles and gets it, but says for him remembering that night still brings back the awful feeling of my being lost and his being responsible. I remind him we were both responsible—the way we both are for the rest of it. He nods; it's the party line. But I don't think at the moment he buys it.

There is definitely a down side to symbiosis: my moods are linked to his, and I don't know how to undo it. If Stone is up and enjoying himself, so am I. If he's down, I am not only down, but frantic as to how to bring him back. And helpless.

There is a lot of helpless.

119

July 10, 1995

God, what is it you want of me, of us? Why are you screwing us over like this? Why do you give Stone good news with one hand and throw something miserable at him with the other?

Kevin gives Stone a colored plastic overlay sheet that makes it possible for him to read much more easily—happily, even. (A certain type of dyslexia responds to this, and apparently Stone has it.)

Stone is exalted in the moment, thrilled with the prospect of getting through as many books as he can, as fast as he can. The world opens a little more (before he knows, it will snap shut) and he is willing, so willing. Then Alan Quartermaine comes in and tells him his T-cells are back down.

Stone plunges. I plunge after him, try to pick him up, dust him off, transfuse hope: Alan will get him this new other drug—experimental—3-TC—It's done wonders for . . . etc.

At least I have Sonny to help. He's as relentless as I am trying to keep Stone standing up and walking. And Stone keeps trying very hard, for both of us. But we are all very tired.

Something I wanted to say to Sonny and finally did: though I'm sure he's aware that early on I tried to discourage Stone from working for him, I'm very glad Stone held out.

Right now I thank God for the presence of Sonny Corinthos in Stone's (and therefore my) life.

July 12, 1995

Speaking of help from unexpected sources.

When Katherine Bell (who nobody I know trusts or likes) asked how Stone was and moved on to Uncle Mac, I thought, I need this? I guess I did.

She asked me to try to see things from Mac's point of view. While I pour all my love and attention into Stone and my impending loss, Mac has a loss, too. What loss? Me, my innocence, maybe my life, possibly my love, which it feels like I've transferred to Stone.

I argue love doesn't work that way; she argues Mac doesn't know that. I argue Stone has no one except Sonny and me. She argues who does Mac have? He's alone, he's afraid, he's reacting badly . . . I get this about Stone, why not about Mac?

How could such a basically awful person as Katherine Bell be right?

I went to Mac and told him I'd been rotten and I missed him and I love him and I really don't want it to be like this for us. So maybe it won't be anymore.

Is that what Stone means about tolerance? I'm just glad to have my "family" again. (And from his speechless embrace, so is Mac.)

July 14, 1995

I guess I forgave Uncle Mac just in time, because today I have to forgive myself.

Stone forgave me first, of course. Instantly. But I will never, ever again ask about anyone: "How could he/she . . . ?"

How could I say the things I did to Stone, the way I said them? Brave faithful good good good Robin? I mean it was one thing to trash Uncle Mac up and down and anyone else who disappointed me, but to yell at Stone, "You're just feeling sorry for yourself. What about me?!"

I hate putting this down and that's why I need to. To review when I feel self-righteous, or sorry for myself.

I kept yelling, couldn't stop. (At Stone. I raised my voice at Stone.) All the things I swore I'd never say, all the questions I'd never ask, all my fear for me, me, me. I called him stupid and careless and how did he know he hadn't given it to me?!

Instant horror, instant shame, Stone's face filled with pain, but not surprise. As if it were what he'd been waiting to hear.

The "mad" he'd been looking for had been there all along. It shocked me much more than it shocked him. And it was an incredible, gushing, broken-open relief.

July 16, 1995

We went for a walk this morning, Elmwood Park, just after dawn, before the heat moved in. When we got to our bench by the fountain, we sat down and were just quiet, close. Kissed the way we did that first time.

It's been a lot different since I blew up at Stone. He was actually glad it happened. Said if I couldn't tell him how I feel, even when it was bad, then things between us would be phony, which they've never been. All that positive stuff was great, but we were both pretty strung out on it. We both seem more real again.

He's still on my case, though, about being too centered on him —reminds me that after all, I'll be going off to Yale next month. I back away from this discussion every time he brings it up, but pretty soon I'm going to have to tell him and Mac what I've decided. (When I do, and I haven't yet.) I know this much: Yale as an institution is going to be here longer than Stone is.

July 18, 1995
General Hospital

Alan Quartermaine pulled some strings and got Stone into the 3-TC program as of today. Alan says over 26,000 AIDS patients have done well on it. I was excited, of course, and said so, and Stone seemed pretty hopeful, too, but I had to cover up what that number did to me: 26,000 AIDS patients—just a small sample of the number there are, and a tiny percentage of the number there have been.

I went to the library early on and looked it up, trying to gather some positive information. There wasn't any. According to my notes, there have been 441,528 cases of AIDS diagnosed and reported since 1981. Of those, 270,870 individuals have died—leaving 170,658 currently living with AIDS.

And currently one of the fastest-growing groups being diagnosed are heterosexual teenagers. Like Stone.

Another of the fastest growing groups: women, particularly minority women.

And AIDS is the leading cause of death of men aged 25 to 30.

That's in this country, mind you. In poor places, like rural Mexico, like Africa, and parts of South America, people either aren't tested because there aren't enough medical facilities or refuse to be tested, refuse to know, refuse to face it.

I think of these people and the people who love them, all of those lives taken over by the disease. People who thought it could never touch them, like Stone and me—who thought they knew all about it, but didn't. Who thought they were protecting themselves but weren't.

I want to shake people—just people walking down the street. I want to go up to them and say, "Oh, you think you don't know anybody with AIDS? Keep ignoring it. You will."

Enough. I'm exceeding my prescribed daily allowance of negativity. Positive doesn't have to be a lie—it's a manner of looking at things.

Alan is very hopeful about 3-TC for Stone and so are we. I think we should have a party to celebrate.

July 19, 1995

No party. The unthinkable has happened. Brenda and Sonny broke up. And of course, because they are individually the people each of us is closest to, Stone and I are in opposite corners. Just when I thought the issue of Sonny was settled and would never come between us again.

I know it sounds bad. Unbelievable: Brenda wearing a wire for the police to try to entrap Sonny into incriminating himself? Obviously something horrible has to have happened for her to do such a thing. She loves Sonny as much as I love Stone. Stone can't think of anything, under any conditions, that could be bad enough for her to betray Sonny like that.

The thing is, I've come to love Sonny, too, and I hate this so much.

July 21, 1995

Sonny's Apartment

Okay, are we even? —Stone yelled at me! I hit that place where he's immovable, even for love of me: loyalty to Sonny. It feels like months ago and we are back fighting the old issues, only now it's so much worse, because of the reality of his AIDS. Danger on top of danger. Only one is definite and the other is something that is a choice.

It's not the fear of more violence that caused the fight, though. It's my reaction to Sonny's lying. I can take anything but lying. Ironic, I guess, given the amount of my own lying I've recorded in this diary, but there is, after all, a question of scale.

It is a very, very large thing for Sonny to have lied to Brenda

123

about what appear to be his real business activities. And it appears the rumors of his connections to organized crime may well be true.

Stone's position: Sonny's been protecting Brenda; what Sonny doesn't want to tell is nobody's business. Brenda could have gotten out of the relationship without betraying him.

<u>What is he saying</u>?! That he condones anything Sonny might be into???

I tell him how I'd feel if he lied to me. He gets defensive and angry, yells "I'm not going to listen to you trash Sonny. Is that clear?!" And he storms into the bathroom and slams the door. I hear him being sick behind it.

I guess he's gone to sleep now. I'm going to wait it out and try again. This is too large and I'm too frightened to let go.

Later

Some things you have to let go anyway. When I was curled up, miserable, on Sonny's couch, Luke came in. I'm not sure if our conversation clarified things or muddied them up worse, but I wound up apologizing to Stone.

I must have sounded pretty self-righteous to Luke—going off on Sonny's morals and ethics (or what I considered to be the lack of) because Luke said for him, such matters were not clear cut.

That it was easier for him to understand Sonny's protecting Brenda than it was her setting up the man she's supposed to love. And all of a sudden I was hearing Daddy again, saying there are no good or bad guys; we all are both.

So I went in and told Stone and promised to shut up about it. The love and gratitude in his face were worth it. I guess we've "agreed to disagree" again. Same subject, same outcome, except we both know that now we haven't got time to be mad at each other.

But I'm still mad at Sonny for what he did to Brenda.

July 22, 1995

Walked in on Mac and Felicia talking, and they suddenly stopped. Turned out they were discussing Stone. Good sign??

Mac mentioned reading about new treatments for AIDS and did Stone know about them. It was the first time he's said anything

<u>close</u> to supportive, and I was slightly stunned but grateful. (Even though anything new takes years to develop, years Stone realistically doesn't have.)

Stone, in the mood he's been in, didn't even tell me that Felicia had taken the trouble to visit him. So sweet of her. She was amazed by his courage and insight. I hope she told him so. He really needs it right now.

What good does it do for me to continually tell Stone he's special? It's just me talking—the woman in love with him. It needs to come from other places, too. I said so, and looked at Mac, but he went to go pour somebody some coffee. I wish he could manage just some small gesture. It would mean so much to Stone. (And to the woman who loves him.)

August 3, 1995
Sharpe Printing

Thought I'd smoothed things over with Stone but he's still uptight and growly. "This is <u>my</u> illness, you don't get to manage it." (This because I bring him sugarless muffins and tell him what I learned about sugar and the immune system.) When he is sarcastic it hurts the most.

I remember reading once that "sarcasm" is derived from the Greek word meaning to tear the flesh. Does that essential piece of information help, Robin? See, now I'm doing the tearing. That's what happens when I feel really helpless and stupid: I beat up on myself. Not bright, maybe, but it's better than beating up on Stone.

I did let him know he'd hurt me, though, kind of whining, which he hated more, and Luke, who'd been listening to our snarking, came down on us for making this tougher on each other. He told Stone to quit taking his anger re the AIDS out on me, and me to pull back on the mother-hen number. But, he said, feel free to ignore him because he doesn't know anything anyway.

I get the feeling this was a reference to Laura. Sometimes I really forget that other people are living lives with problems. Maybe not as dramatic as AIDS, but they still have to deal.

Fortunately (fine timing) at that point Jason came in to ask Luke to sponsor a team on the AIDS walk Sunday and Luke grabbed hold and got us all working together (including Stone), so now I wait for the rush-order T-shirts. I certainly hope they meet with his approval.

Later, 11:00 P.M.
Home

Stone apologized later on and I could see it really hurt him to have hurt me. The hardest thing for him to deal with right now are the mood swings. The physical stuff he expects and is more or less on top of (for now, anyway), but the emotional change-ups are weird for him.

He's always been pretty even-tempered, and I guess I liked that about him from the first. (I get this weird vision of the virus forming teams and throwing their weight around in his head.) He says it's like living inside a stranger. I stopped myself from saying it's the same for me—only the stranger is outside.

Just the moment for him to bring up Yale and how it will be good for me to get away and make a space for myself. So I couldn't put off telling him anymore: no way am I going to Yale in three weeks. (Did he really think I'd leave him now?)

He is appalled and angry and guilty and very worried about how Mac will react. Do I honestly want to stick around and watch him die? (I flash on the end of summer last year, worrying ahead if

AIDS
Walk in the Park '95

Sponsor Pledge Form

Name _____

Address _____

City/State/Zip _____ Home _____ |

Phone: Work _____ |

Help us reach our goal of $100 per wal

Sponsor's Name	Pledge per Km
	$25.
1	
2	
3	
4	
5	
6	

For more info call: 1-800-555

126

"we" could survive my going away to school eventually. His ambition to be something more for me. My growing sureness that we could make anything work.)

Now I tell him the only precious thing in my life is whatever time we have together. If and when he dies I will be right there beside him.

It's my life, and he doesn't get to manage it. Later on I told Uncle Mac the same thing.

August 5, 1995
Post-AIDS Walk

A little like the night of my Yale acceptance: everyone I run into either knows or finds out in front of me that I'm not going. Courtesy, naturally, of Uncle Mac Scorpio.

Careful, measured, of-course-it's-your-life-but-have-you-really-thought-it-through's. But most seem to understand when I explain it. Except for Mac, who of course blames Stone, and Stone, who still blames himself. And I refuse to discuss it with either one of them.

What would I say— that the great fund of human knowledge will wait for me? That lectures and research and intellectual exploration will be useful to fill the big black void that will be in my head and my heart

afterwards? (No. No! Stone will always be there. Stone will always be for me. Please, please don't let me think about this now. It will wait. It will keep.)

How can I miss one instant of actually, physically being near him? Of feeling his skin, his hair, his voice, his doing or saying anything?

I keep wondering what it meant, all those people in the park proclaiming sympathy on their sponsored T-shirts. —Do they have a clue??? Of course they do. Who am I to belittle them? Maybe it's only an expression of helplessness, all those individuals walking to raise money that amounts to a drop in the bucket. But they are there, and they raise a little consciousness. Comradeship. Jon Hanley, looking fitter than ever, passes by Stone and me and waves. I push back a stab of envy and fear that Jon will be here longer because he knew sooner and has had more time to do the right things.

Interesting how the negative thoughts sneak up. (Like the virus.) When does negative become realistic? I still hear Alan's voice when I don't want to, saying, "a virulent strain."

And there is something as virulent as the virus—what Jon spoke about at the Ball. Deadly, free-falling hate.

We ran into it at the Walk, and Stone went after it (like going into a dark hole after a snake). He overheard a woman complaining to her friend that "they" had taken over the whole park—that maybe "they" should all die and get it over with. That in her opinion "those people have gotten exactly what they deserve."

I was struck dumb, but Stone confronted her politely: Did she mean people with AIDS? They deserve it, as a punishment?

Yes, she allowed, that's what she meant.

Whereupon he asked what he'd done to deserve it and who was punishing him.

Oh, she was truly God's-on-my-side, actually saying to his face it's probably because of his immoral, sinful behavior. Perverting natural and divine law.

I am ready to pounce on her, and pummel her: <u>Whose</u> law, bitch?! Who do you think . . . how do you dare, etc., but Jason holds me back, makes me let Stone handle it, which he does, so simply and beautifully I've never had more pride in him.

128

He was taught God loved him, he says, that he was made in God's image, and he can't quite imagine God's wanting this to happen to him.

The bitch says he can't presume to know what God wants. But she's presuming, he points out. Does she know anyone with AIDS—does she have a clue what it's about? She grabs her friend and rushes off. I hope Stone will haunt her heart forever.

"Blessed are they that hunger and thirst after righteousness." Not the self-righteous. I wonder if they'll all be surprised when they meet each other in Hell.

August 10, 1995

But there are other, graceful people, and people who change in some way because of it all.

Like Laura Spencer, who doesn't run in panic at Stone's blood flowing from a gash he gets trying to help Lucky with his go-cart. Doesn't chase the children away, handles it simply, carefully, intelligently.

And more astounding, A.J. Quartermaine—yes, A.J.—who is so moved by Stone's response to the devil-lady in the park that he sits down and writes a thoughtful, loving, astonishing letter of admiration and thanks for what Stone's teaching him.

August 14, 1995

Something allows us to still have routines—I spend time at the Charles Street Foundation, fill in at the Outback when needed, do a few household chores, mostly laundry. (There's something satisfying about laundry, like it's something you can solve.)

When Stone is working and I'm not, I spend time with Felicia, sometimes spelling her with the girls. (Maxie's become quite a good little diver, thank you. I hold Georgie at the edge of the pool and trail her feet in the water.)

I'd spend more time with Brenda, but she seems to be spending most of hers with Miguel, "rehearsing." (A euphemism, at least part of the time, for screwing around.) Stone thought from the start there was more going on than I wanted to believe, but now they really flaunt being lovers.

I try not to be judgmental—I know it's all rebound stuff and she's hurting—but something in me is a little repulsed. I suppose because I can't imagine loving one man and hopping into bed with another. Truthfully, and I try not to think about it, I can't imagine making love with anyone other than Stone, ever.

Stone when he's not doing stuff for Sonny (some of the jobs I'm sure Sonny manufactures for him) is working out faithfully, helping Lucky with the go-cart, and doing a lot of reading, which is still a trip for him, thanks to Kevin's magic overlay.

He's probably done too much, because he's complaining of eye strain, but try to get him to stop. He reads everything, with a great lack of snobbery, and a lot of wonder. Now he wants to get colored glasses that will enable him to write as well as read.

I try not to apply "at least he can" to these things. This is life, minute by minute, and there is a lot of joy in it. And even some hope for more, because the great news is, his T-cells are up again, due apparently to the 3-TC in combination with AZT.

August 20, 1995

I haven't been able to write in here for days because I couldn't stand to. It is beyond thinking or accepting, beyond committing the words to a page. Beyond tolerating or understanding on any level:

Stone's in the hospital, a catheter in his vein allowing the slow drip three times a day of yet another medicine. This one's called gancyclovir. Its purpose is to slow the destruction of Stone's vision. Right, slow, not stop.

His "eyestrain?" CMV. One of AIDS' many packages of good-ies. An infection called cytomegalovirus that destroys the retina. Not uncommon. His eye doctor says maybe half of all Americans contract it in their lifetime and fight it off without ever knowing. But those people have working immune systems.

In other words, Stone is going blind. They give him, at best, 105 days of sight left, even with the medicine.

I would scream at God, but why bother?

Stone, reeling from it, at first considers yanking the tube from his arm, going downstairs, and walking directly into traffic. What stops him is the knowledge he'd probably cause a bad accident

130

and maybe kill someone besides himself. He is hurting as much from <u>our</u> pain for him (mine and Sonny's and everyone's) as from his, worries terribly about draining us of energy and spirit (and in the case of Sonny, the enormous cost of the accumulating medical bills).

Sonny assures him it's okay, more than okay, that paying those bills makes him feel useful. For me there isn't any choice. You put your energy where the love is. Stone's using this time in that blank room where there are few images to memorize, to keep reading. Sometimes we read to each other, which is a new kind of pleasure. Even now, in the middle of this awfulness, new good things.

August 21, 1995

I've tried to take the only positive step I could think of—something I've had brewing awhile.

A.J.'s letter had cheered Stone up so much I got the idea of putting together a kind of memory book for him. Asking everyone to contribute something—letters, poems, pictures, stories, anything we can put between covers that will show how we feel about him. Maybe stuff to remind him of things they've done together—or to make him laugh.

I think it will give people a way to say things to him they maybe would feel uncomfortable saying. And give

Stone in "anti-dyslexia" glasses

Stone something tangible to see while he can see—and remember when he can't.

August 24, 1995

Comic relief: A day at the beach, compliments of three dear goofy friends. Stone and I are hanging out in his GH room (like we have a choice) when A.J. pokes his head around the door, looking like an extra-terrestrial in wrap-around shades and a wild Hawaiian

shirt and is followed into the room by Keesha and Jason, done up beachlike, just as crazily, all carrying a ton of equipment and picnic stuff.

They explain it is sweltering out, the rays beating down, the perfect day for the beach, and since Stone can't get there, they've brought him carry-out. Not just carry-out food, carry-out <u>beach</u>.

They even have—would you believe?— sand, which they spread lightly on a plastic ground cloth, hand Stone a pail and shovel, blast the Beachboys and get out a magnificent picnic banquet. They have brought hats and sunglasses for Stone and me.

We buy into this insanity very fast—so great to see Stone laugh like that (for <u>himself</u>, instead of someone else's benefit) and to soak up the love and friendship. Also for the first time in months be ravenously hungry, eat <u>a lot</u>, and not throw up.

For further entertainment, A.J. has brought a selection of Beach Blanket movies of the early sixties—examples of what the young people who <u>weren't</u> hippies were doing—which was being incredibly innocent while jiggling around in fairly chaste bikinis, singing duets, and playing volley ball. (Those were the days.)

Thank you, dear crazy friends. We love you, too.

August 25, 1995

More friends, more caring, more visits, and a few conflicts. Brenda and Miguel arrive and while Stone is glad to see them, can't help being uncomfortable because of his loyalty to Sonny, and finally says so. (I love and admire his honesty so much, his refusal to "make nice.")

To give them credit, Miguel and Brenda don't walk out wounded. They say they still want to be his friends and support him. Stone realizes he wants and needs this, too—it's no time to turn his back on anyone who cares about him.

I guess they "agree to disagree."

But then apparently Sonny turned up and there was more awkwardness. He and Brenda went out in the hall, and when she came back she said they'd worked out a way to deal with the situation and still all support Stone. Sonny came back later and said the same thing, more or less. But Stone could see both of them are still in awful pain over each other. And their pain hurts him.

Then there's the business of Jagger. Felicia, when she visited, encouraged Stone to tell him and Karen about his condition. Stone insists not yet.

I know he feels he let his brother down by getting AIDS, that it's the final "gift" of the street life Jagger despised so much for him. He's expecting a huge "I told you so," but anyone who knows Jagger knows better. I guess Stone doesn't understand he's the one saying it to himself. And depriving himself, as well as Jagger.

Unreasonable as this is, we have to respect it. If he couldn't protect himself, he wants to protect his brother as long as he can. Selfishly, I wish he would call them. It would mean a lot to get a hug from Karen right now.

August 27, 1995

Okay, okay. There's no need to panic.

How many times in my life have I come down with a sore throat and swollen glands and a fever? At least a dozen. Maybe two. Run-of-the-mill, garden-variety stuff everybody gets. Ordinary, ache-all-over, take-two-aspirin-and-get-into-bed sick is all I am.

They got worried about the way I looked at the office, and when I said how I felt, Jason yanked me over to his father's office over my protests. Possible strep. Alan did a throat culture—and drew blood for another HIV. I may be able to avoid Mac, but I have to tell Stone why I can't come see him for twenty-four hours. Alan gave me antibiotics. They will knock it out of me.

I'll call Stone, then crawl into bed and drink liquids.

Called him

Worse than I thought. He freaked, terrified he's given It to me. His AIDS started with the same symptoms. So, I pointed out, do a lot of things. Like simple strep, which I've been prone to since I was a kid.

He asked if Alan had done an HIV test. Of course, I say brightly. Routine. Results tomorrow.

Later

Mac just left. I couldn't avoid him. He came home early and found me in bed at seven o'clock at night and knew right away something was up. He tried hard not to panic in front of me, agreed it was probably what Alan said, and proceeded to hold me so tight I could hardly breathe.

I'm still not sure what the best way is to deal with fear. Is it better to acknowledge it and stare it down or keep stomping on it? Either way it's there, and so is the bug in my body, whatever its name may be.

August 28, 1995

A miracle: one of those strange turn-arounds where something bad ultimately brings about something fine. Mac seems to be having a change of heart about Stone.

It was my being sick that did it, and his seeing Stone in a state of miserable guilt and raw terror over what might happen to me. Mac said all of a sudden it was like looking in a mirror, and he realized they were sharing the same suffering, the same fear for me.

Stone told me, and I tremble when I think of it, that Mac put his arms around him and held him.

August 30, 1995

Surprise visitor to Stone: Lucy Coe. He was sounding a little dazed from it when I called. He thought at first she was lost and was clearly flattered when he realized she meant to be there.

He recognizes her as an original and obviously enjoyed her visit. A lot. Hey. (That was a jealous pang.)

Well, I guess I should be grateful he's still in shape to react to her God-knows-considerable appeal.   Besides, I really have to like Lucy. She's so . . . original. So Lucy Coe. Mainly, I appreciate her because she appreciates Stone and let him know it.

She wants to give a dinner party for us when he gets out of the hospital! Just a few friends and her duck. (As a guest, that is, not the entree.) Really sweet.

As much as I love and am grateful for what everyone's doing, there is something sad in me that wonders what life would have been like for Stone if he'd gotten the kind of love and caring he's getting now when he was small?

Later

I'm negative. I'm alright. It's not <u>It</u>. It really is only strep.

When Alan called with the results, I about collapsed in Mac's arms. We've pledged not to spend the next two months till my next blood test in terror over this thing. I refuse to quake every time I get the sniffles.

The best was telling Stone. When I did there was this silence over the phone. Palpable joy and relief. Funny, I remember when finding out you had a strep throat was bad news.

I have to stay away from him for five more hours, till I'm officially not contagious. Strep would be more than bad news for him. It could kill him. (Sooner rather than later.)

September 1, 1995

Uncle Mac came by to see Stone and brought him dinner from the Outback. It was brief and awkward but touching. When he left, Stone and I stared at each other, with tears and amazement.

September 6, 1995

Stone's out! He's home. His eyes are better (well, "the rate of degeneration is stabilized"—per Alan), and we can get about the business of cramming everything we can into the rest of the time he has to see. Somewhere around three months. He's opted for oral treatment (cheesh, more pills?) rather than going in to GH for a daily drip. Figures he'd rather have the time this would take for himself while he still feels able to use it. Of course, if he keeps fit and does everything right he should stay well for a long time, well beyond the loss of his vision. And I know he'll deal.

He already is. Right now he told Alan he wants to burn images into his memory—everything—"trees, flowers, paintings, dogs, clouds, birds, skylines." He grinned and said he'd add beautiful women but there's no room for any face but mine in his head.

When we got back to Sonny's place, it took all the restraint I could dig up not to start "organizing" this project for him. God, however much I love him and want for him, please let me let him be. Allow him to do for himself while he still can.

Maybe God was ahead of that prayer because he brought Mike in with a model airplane and they got all revved about making one together. A big radio-controlled job, something they've both always wanted. We'll take it to Elmwood Park to fly, and we can look at clouds at the same time. Two for one.

September 8, 1995

In what is probably the opposite of poetic justice, Sonny has bought Tiffany and Sean's old place. He and Stone seem to think this is screamingly funny: living in the former abode of the chief of police. An irony I'd rather not comprehend in detail.

But Sonny took Stone and Luke and me over to inspect their new digs, and really I'm glad it's happening. I never thought I'd be in that apartment again, and I always loved it a lot.

Stone likes the idea of living in a place where I've lived from time to time, and he chose my old room for his own. You can see the lake from the window, and the docks where he used to hang out before he had an address.

I suspected leaving his room at Sonny's must be kind of a wrench, and he admitted it. It's the first place he'd ever had in his life that he could call his own. I think the first place he ever felt safe. But he realized it was Sonny who actually made him a home, and Sonny's the one he's moving with, so . . .

Improbable, but there it all is.

Later—midnight

Mac and Sonny being at the same party and keeping the peace is pretty improbable too, but they were and they did tonight. Being, not exactly jolly with each other, but at least civil for Stone's and my sake.

Luke, who used to enjoy Mac's company, is at odds with him, too, and points out if Mac gets his way and manages to put Sonny behind bars, what happens to Stone? This is a heavy question I can't even think about, but I hope Mac is.

Still, the party was joyful, Lucy a very Gracious Lady, and Kevin emanating as much warmth as I've ever seen him allow himself in public. Were we talking Improbable? How about them as a couple? Hey, how about me and Stone as a couple?? I guess Improbables attract.

Lucy made a sweet toast about Stone and celebrating life and Stone made one back, grateful and loving everybody and really getting it that they love him. He said he never expected it and I said a very loud and public I told you so.

Incredible warmth, love, and a lot of laughing by Us, Lucy and Kevin, Keesha, Jason, A.J. Sonny, Lily, Luke, Felicia, Uncle Mac, and Sigmund. Conspicuously not there:

Brenda and Miguel, which was sad, but probably for the best.

Lucy panicked at one point, realizing there'd be thirteen at table, which is supposed to attract ill fortune (Grandma Fil always said that, too), but Kevin said he didn't think it counted if one was a duck.

September 13, 1995

We're moving Stone into his new room at Uncle Sean's today. (It will take some adjusting for me to call that apartment anything else.)

I just realized, remembering things, how much I'll miss Stone's old room, too. Picnics on the floor, lots of time in bed. A lot of discovery happening . . . Better stop right there. If I start in that direction, I'll wind up feeling depressed and deprived.

But if I don't, where will that energy go? What do I do with the pain and the missing that part of us? If I can't say it here, where can I? Okay: It's Not Fair. We knew that; it's a given. (Newsflash: Doesn't make it easier.) It's not fair. We had only just started, and there was so much lovemaking to do. If I remember us in Stone's room, in Stone's bed . . . .

I get very sick of this sublimating! Stone is still here, and those feelings are as alive as all the rest of our loving. (More alive, maybe, from being ignored.) We weren't going to let fear ruin the time we have.

We weren't going to be stupid, either.

"Virulent," remember?

But I miss being held and touched. I miss just lying, skin next to skin with him. I miss feeling drunk on each other.

And writing this all down is driving me up the wall!!!

I have to do something about this. Research?

Later, 10 P.M.
The Move

A.J. and Jason and I got the boxes from Sonny's while Stone started organizing things on the other end. I tried not to give him too many controlling suggestions.

He'd set up a hospitality bar (soda, etc.) and had fun playing host to the three of us. When we got there he was about to scarf down his humongous number of pills, which he made into a wonderful, funny performance, lining them all up, identifying and swallowing them with a great flourish.

I guess my attitude about Stone's brand of humor has improved. I figure, who am I to tell him how to cope? Jason and I thought the whole number was hysterical, but A.J. was shocked into an astounding realization: Stone has AIDS. Yup. He really does. A.J., who, for a Quartermaine, is a little lacking in social grace, said if he were in Stone's shoes he'd probably drive off a bridge. Jason was mortified, but Stone was very matter of fact—said he'd thought of it, but minute by minute he was still enjoying himself, and his friends, who even include A.J.

Klutzy as he is, I still have A.J. to thank for my memory book project, and I'm making a lot of progress. Asked Luke today, and he's happy to contribute.

Speaking of progress . . .

Before the move I stopped over at the GH AIDS Outreach project, asked for a counselor, and boldly put forth my questions. (Don't know why I didn't do this before. What did I think, we were the first people to have this problem?) She was great—straight-talking, unembarrassed, specific. What's safe, what isn't. Protection, always. Would you believe, she actually had pamphlets! (Full of funny jargon: "alternative behaviors," "rethinking intimacy," and my personal favorite: "outercourse!") Figured if nothing else it would make Stone laugh. So I took two copies and slipped Stone's under his pillow when I made up his bed. I hope he has trouble sleeping.

September 14, 1995

I arrived, rather shamelessly, at 8:00 A.M. Let myself in with my old Sean-Tiff key. (Sonny'd said by all means to keep it and use it.) Knocked and poked my head into Stone's room. He was asleep, but the pamphlet was on the floor next to the bed. I undressed and crawled in with him.

September 16, 1995

It feels like only Stone and I understand about time. Everybody else thinks they have it spread out in front of them indefinitely.

140

Stone tried to point this out to Sonny, and tell him how much Brenda's actually hurting. (He <u>knows</u> how much Sonny is.)

We were celebrating Jason's birthday at Kelly's. (Getting to be Party Central around here.) This time Brenda and Miguel were included and Sonny and Lily weren't—they have no relationship with Jason, after all—but as Sonny was bringing Lily home, they ran into Brenda and Miguel on the stairs in what used to be called a "compromising position."

It got a little ugly, and Sonny turned around and took Lily home with <u>him</u>, making it very clear they are lovers after all.

Now I'm really ticked at Sonny for pulling Stone into this. Like Stone doesn't feel helpless enough. I don't know if asking him to deliver a message to Brenda ("come and get the boxes you left at the apartment") was cowardice or another way to hurt her, but she wound up crying her eyes out in Stone's arms, and now he feels responsible somehow for fixing things.

He can't stand seeing people he loves and knows still love each other screwing up and wasting their precious time, and it hurts him that this may not be resolved before he has to "check out." I hope he conveyed <u>that</u> to Sonny. Maybe Sonny will swallow his pride for Stone.

September 18, 1995

Michael Stone Cates jumped off a bridge tonight.

Fortunately, he was attached to a bungee cord.

This madness started when Luke was encouraging him to think of things he's always wanted to do—and do them. Now. (I.e., while you can.) I thought this was great when he was saying he always wanted to learn to ski, but <u>bungee jumping</u>? What is my problem, he asks, afraid I'll break my neck and die? Very funny, I say, but I have to laugh and Luke says, okay, let's go! Now? Now.

Luke has a friend who has equipment, Luke knows how to use it, before we know it we're out on Port Charles Bridge in the black of night, Stone in a harness and already on such a high he's barely scared, so of course I'm scared for both of us. Luke assures us he's got the whole thing under control, and I am trying hard not to remember that Laura left him because of his love affair with danger.

It is so dark you can't even see the water. You can't even see the bridge! Luke tosses a rock over the railing and it is a <u>long time</u>

before we hear the splash. I am further terrified; Stone is elated. I say, kind of desperately, "I love you." He shouts back, "I love you, Robin" as he leaps out into the black night air.

It was like flying, he said, except better. The dark and the drop, and at the bottom soaring back into the air again, his hair wet from his head's touching the water. Totally letting go, totally sure of absolutely nothing and not caring. Luke pulls him back up over the railing, all of us laughing crazily, half-crying, hugging, full of having defied death for the moment.

September 19, 1995

So we are at Kelly's and Stone is now truly into this live-your-fantasies thing, and I grab a napkin and start to make a list, and he grabs it back and says he will make it, because believe it or not he has never made a list of anything in his life. (He has this really sharp detailed memory I guess he developed because he found it so hard to write.)

So he puts on his glasses and starts to make a list, and I pledge to make everything on it happen—until I see his next heart's desire: swim with dolphins??? What is this, inspired by reruns of "Flipper"?

No, inspired by the sheer poetry of the idea, I think. He doesn't say this, but I can tell, from the way he describes it—swim with them, get one to trust him, ride its back. All of a sudden I really want to make this happen for him.

I guess I can start with the local aquarium. Only thing, I point out, is that Stone doesn't know how to swim, and has up till now refused my advances at teaching him. Now he consents. It's too late for the beach, but there's always the Quartermaine pool, or the Y. Perfectly possible.

Further desires: see a shooting star, walk on stilts, go hang gliding, take a trip on an airplane (honestly, he never has), see the sunrise with me from the top of the tallest building in town. All arrangeable. He'll think of more, don't worry.

We are really into it, and all of a sudden, as happens so often now, his mood takes a 180. Not down, but serious. Fantasies are great, he says, but what he really wants more than ever is to make up for the time we won't have together . . . having babies and growing old, watching me get grey hair (and, I tease him, you lose yours).

And especially Christmases. He's never had what he calls a real Christmas—even when he was a little kid with Jagger and Gina (the family being not exactly the Waltons)—with a real tree that drops needles, carols, a big Christmas dinner. I am suddenly washed over, wanting that too, wanting to make him that dinner with all the trimmings.

It's like this a lot now, times of great pleasure and hilarity, sharper because of the looming loss, which all of a sudden raises its head and causes a chill, like a ghost, in advance.

He takes my hand and tells me it's okay, every day is Christmas with me. But he wants to give me something, something to keep when he's gone, to remember him by. I tell him I'll never need anything more than his love, that I'll have the whole rest of my life.

I have a sudden feeling of my head grazing the top of black water. The bungee cord pulls me back: Stone decides to pursue his most accessible, immediate fantasy—building the largest ice cream sundae ever known to humankind.

September 20, 1995

It is so precious and so beautiful and so perfect. He said it was at the top of his wish list and he did it: got me something wonderful to remember him—an exquisite antique cameo ring. I look at it and see a century of other love stories. Timeless, like us. It will always be the most cherished thing I own—except for the memory of Stone's face when he gave it to me.

September 21, 1995

Walk-on-stilts day. Jason and Keesha, Miguel and Brenda come to the park with us, bring a picnic. The moment arrives, Stone stares at the stilts, openly apprehensive. We all think this is a scream: he bungee jumps in the dark and he's afraid of stilts?

That's the answer, he says, wait till night falls so nobody can see him make a total fool of himself. I point out if everyone waited for that, nothing would ever get done in this world.

We help him onto the stilts and I burst out laughing: he definitely does look absolutely ridiculous. Nothing personal, I assure him. Anybody would. And crack up again.

He teeters and takes a couple of steps, then gets over-confi-dent and takes a misstep, and crashes down onto the ground. I rush over, afraid what I'm hearing is sobs and he's broken some-thing, and find he is actually shaking with laughter. I offer to help him onto them again. No need. Some experiences you only have to have once, thank you.

He pulls me down with him and we lie there dissolving in laughter and idiot pleasure.

September 22, 1995

He ran into Jon Hanley today, volunteering at Ward House—Jon's way of honoring his lover, Greg, who died five years ago. Was able to thank Jon for what he'd said at the Nurses' Ball and tell him it had helped him go public with his AIDS. Jon's parting word of advice was: <u>live</u>.

Exactly what we are doing, fiercely in-the-moment. Stone looks and a lot of the time feels fantastic. Since the hospital, he's been working out regularly, and his body . . . don't get me started. I see him in amazement, gulping down experiences and at the same time <u>watching</u> everything, making a record of it. I feel his eyes on me, memorizing. (I try not to notice I am doing the same to him.)

Today, as part of the GH AIDS Outreach Program, he spoke to kids at Charles Street School about how he got AIDS, what it meant, how to protect themselves. (Alan told me later he was wonderful: straightforward, honest, sobering.)

Stone was glad he'd done it but frustrated and worried by some of the attitudes he encountered—a girl afraid to protect her-self because her boyfriend didn't like condoms, the boyfriend arro-gant, unwilling to hear. Lazy? Rebellious? Adolescent-invincible? Stupid, is what Stone said, in their face.

More stupidity: On the way out a kid who hadn't been there but had heard he had AIDS sauntered by Stone and called him "faggot." Lucky Spencer, who was there (Emily, too) told me Stone was "awesomely cool," quietly asking the kid what he meant, and calmly giving him hell on behalf of Jon Hanley and a lot of other decent, loving people.

144

Can it be Michael Cates is finally getting a sense that he's a good person? I hope so. I wish it hadn't taken this to show him.

September 23, 1995

The school incident bothers me more and more.

This homophobia.

Why is it people are so afraid of "other"? Why is anyone's way of loving anyone else's business?

And even if they believe it's wrong in the eyes of God (presumptuous as that is), what about compassion, what about empathy? What happened to "let he who is without sin," etc.?

"They brought it on themselves" is what the devil-lady and her friends say. Oh, right. So how come we don't judge and reject people with cancer or emphysema from smoking, or people with heart disease from gumming up their arteries with fat, or, for that matter, people who drown from swimming out too far???

How dare anyone, <u>anyone</u>, dismiss a whole segment of society, disregard massive suffering, loss, pain? Hate must be a major anesthetic.

But suppose, just suppose, God sent this thing in this way to test our compassion, our humanity, our charity?

Some people are going to be in big trouble.

September 25, 1995

Can't, won't focus. Don't want to write. T-cells down again— to 53. (My mind takes the weirdest turns: there is a musical theme in my head I can't place. Finally identify it as Haydn's "Farewell Symphony" . . . the one where little by little the musicians leave the stage until it is totally quiet.)

Alan: 3-TC/AZT has worked well for some. But not, it seems, for Stone. What now? Protease inhibitors? (Stone's been <u>reading</u>.) Blockbuster drugs. Alan: <u>very</u> experimental, can prolong life two or more years. Stone has a flash of hope that burns out fast. Not only very $$$ (which surely could be managed, somehow), but he's not eligible. Why? Something about liver tests, other aspects.

Down to the wire.

Suggested new regimen: foscarnet and D4T, intravenous. Means a daily visit to the hospital, another catheter, a daily drip of some other kind of supposed hope into his veins.

He comes to tell me at the Outback. We can't do anything but look at each other and love each other. He has decided, though, that it's time to call his brother.

September 26, 1995, 3:00 A.M.

I wake up cold. Stay in the moment. Don't want to. Not this moment. Something all over me, inside and out. Cellular fear.

Adrenalin rush, as though I'm on a track and a train is coming, but the rush doesn't take me away, doesn't help me run. I am frozen with it. Can't move. There is no place away from it: Stone really will die. He really will leave me. His body will stop. Mine will stay here (for a while). I will stop being able to talk to him or touch him.

They will have to take care of his body: burn it or bury it. Stone. What makes him Stone? What makes a person a person?

When you think of a person you get a kind of memory sense of them: how the air feels around them; how they change it by being there. But you can feel this without them, too. What is that? What is that thing? A thought pattern? Brain waves? Some cells give out?

What happens to thinking when you die? What happens to feeling? What happens to the sense between me and Stone? That beautiful, beautiful connection. I can't bear for it to go. How it feels to think about him. How it feels to be able to go to that and reach it and touch it. Where does that go? Please don't take it away. Please. Please. Please make this stop. Grandma, Mother, Daddy, Mac, God—somebody keep him here. Help me.

Morning

I guess I lost it a little last night. The feeling is still with me, but in a duller way. Just a heavy solid truth in the bottom of my stomach.

Stone was right: up to now both of us down deep expected a miracle. Every dip and come back of the T-cells was proof it could happen. Nobody said this. All we said was keep a positive attitude. (And surely we will be rewarded with a miracle.)

No miracle. It's happening; it's closer. Take a breath, and be here. Don't let the fact take space it isn't entitled to. Stone is alive, still, now. Still warm, touchable, connected. Thank God Jagger and Karen are coming.

September 27, 1995

They're here. Stone, whose fear has been building since he made the call, is relaxed and so relieved, having taken Jagger aside and told him. Jagger is shaken but steady, no trace of blame: I'm your brother, I love you, what can I do? The answer is nothing. He did what Stone needed by coming. He calls in Karen, who's appalled <u>for</u> Stone, not <u>at</u> him, as he'd feared.

We all hold each other. We are family.

What makes a family, I wonder. I remember an old "Sesame Street" number with varying combinations of Muppets singing: a grandmother and child, a mixed bunch of kids with two uncles, a single mom and two offspring, an elderly couple. All sing, the gist being no matter the combination, "we're a family." Stone's family came when he asked them. Maybe you don't even have to be related. Maybe a family is just the people who come when we ask them.

Jagger and Karen, with heavy work and school pressures, can't stay more than overnight. They ask Stone to come home with them (unsaid: to die). Stone is touchingly grateful but says no, his life is here. (Unsaid: Robin is here; Sonny is here.)

They offer to take leaves, come here and stay (until . . .). Stone won't let them disrupt their lives. He likes it that they're happy where they are.

But you can see he's at peace, no longer hiding from the brother he was afraid he'd let down. Jagger, when he found out, felt he was the one who'd done the letting down—not finding Stone in time, not fixing things. I think they got it straight with each other.

Jagger wants Stone to call Gina, but Stone's reluctant. She hasn't kept in touch, has never forgiven him for a lot of things. (Like being young and ignorant and not having the good luck to be adopted by doting snobs.) Still, he promises Jagger he'll make the effort. Jagger's sure she won't let him down.

October 6, 1995

She is a monstrous, self-serving, cold-hearted little witch. How could she do it?

How could she hurt him so? He comes to her dying, and she can't handle it? She's sorry he's sick, but she can't help, and her adoptive parents couldn't deal with the concept of her brother (whom they do not remember fondly) having AIDS.

It took Stone so much to call her; he only did it for Jagger. Down deep he knew she wouldn't be there if he asked, but the pain is awful.

I walk in on it and I go out after her, and all I can say is I hope that at some point in her life she desperately profoundly needs love, and someone treats her the way she just treated her brother.

It's okay, Stone. You have all kinds of family. I'm going to start planning the party and the presentation of the memory book.

October 10, 1995

I resent every moment I have to spend anywhere but with him. But I still have to give him space, and because he worries that I have no life except for him, I have to act as if I do. So, most mornings I go to the Charles Street Foundation office and pretend to be there. I watch people getting new starts and chances at what they've wanted for years. I watch A.J. and Keesha administer dreams-come-true, and I enter them in the computer. And I try, really hard, not to ask God why them and not us. (Because I suspect God probably doesn't know.)

October 12, 1995

Happy Birthday To Me

I am eighteen. I went downtown and finally, legally re-obtained my learner's permit to drive.

Standing in line I got a flash of us streaming along in Sonny's Jag, way over the speed limit, till the flashing red gumballs came up behind us.

October 13, 1995

Hey, that was supposed to be Stone's party! And he thought it was supposed to be mine. (Uncle Mac is so totally pleased with himself!)

They really set us up, all our friends. We creep down the path to the Quartermaine boathouse, each thinking the other one is in for the surprise, and all of a sudden there are lights and fireworks and everybody bouncing out at us and it's for both of us. My birthday, Stone's book.

149

Both of us wiped out. I give Stone the book. He is so moved by the letters and contributions (a feather from Sigmund!) he finally has to stop the reading for fear of crying in front of everyone for the rest of the night. For me, so many wonderful, thoughtful, careful gifts, from people who seem to know who I am. But the best gift for both of us was the overwhelming, shining, in-your-face <u>love</u>.

✓ MAKE a LIST & FINNISH IT

✓ BUNGE JUMP
✓ SWIM w/ DOLPHINS *
✓ WALK ON STILTS
✓ FLY IN a PLANE
✓ CAMP OUT ONTOP HI BUILDING
   WATCH SUNRIZE w/ROBIN
✓ WORLDS BIGGEST SUNDAY
✓ SEE SHOOTIGN STAR
✓✓ GET SOMTHING FOR ROBIN- THAT LASTS

* *I think it's fair to check this, too.*

October 14, 1995

Who would have thought a few months back that I'd be capable of feeling bad for A.J.? It was so brave of him even to be there for us last night. And hideously unfair that the first thing he's ever felt personally proud of in his life, the first time he's ever worked hard at anything that wasn't strictly for his own benefit, has blown up in his face.

A total setup, apparently, resulting in ugly scandal for the Charles Street Foundation, and forcing his resignation. Life is so damned unfair. (What else is new?)

And in the middle of all this, A.J. arranges for us to spend the night on the ELQ Building roof tonight. Really touching, how much pleasure it gave him. I guess when you're feeling rottenest about yourself is a good time to do something for somebody.

Late—In the Night
ELQ Roof

So he got us a key to the executive floor here (the tallest building in town, as specified on Stone's list) and arranged with the guard to let us up to the roof. The guard didn't even raise an eyebrow over our camping gear. A Quartermaine has spoken; why should he presume to question? (Even one in disfavor.)

So here we are, camped out. Stone laughed when he saw I'd brought this diary, but I want him to be able to sleep a little and I want to stay awake, so I thought it would give me something to do. Unsaid but understood: I want to keep a record because I can't keep him. I brought a major flashlight-lantern but won't need it—there's a yellow roof light that's plenty. (Also a red blinking one, to warn airplanes, I guess.)

I made us a midnight camp supper, trying to duplicate, without saying so, our famous camp-out dinner the Night of the Bear. Couldn't build a fire up here so brought a camp stove for the pigs-in-blankets. Wondered if he'd remember. He did, of course. They tasted just as good. Better. This time we even got to the s'mores, which wound up in the bear last time.

We zipped the sleeping bags together into a big one, got in, and lay there together looking at the sky. The sunrise we came for is a long time off. You can't see too many stars from here because of the light from the city, but you know they're there.

I ask Stone how he likes camping, now that we've finally gotten to it. Good, he says, and yawns. Then, without a beat, "We'll have to take the kids next time." What kids? Wondering if he means Maxie and Lucas. Ours, he says. I stare. You know . . . Anna and . . . Michael? No, too many Michaels, he mumbles . . . Jason? Alan? Robert? I finally get it and say, what about Sonny? "You sure?" he asks, and grins. I tell him I can live with it. And we go on, playing a game of Future, which is wonderful, because when you know it's not going to happen, you can make it perfect. You can call a kid Sonny Malcolm and be sure he won't get teased about it.

Sonny-Mac Cates is five and Anna Karen is three. No, Stone insists. The girl should be older. Why? So she can set an example for her brother—like you did for me. I disagree, knowing with all my heart it is the other way around, but concede the point.

When is this? Eight, maybe ten years? What do you do? Music business. Executive producer. L & B? No, M & R. I used to go on the road but stopped when the kids started coming. Oh, by the way, you're pregnant again. Again? Didn't we use protection? Well, we were in a big hurry. But the only thing that happened was another baby. There's a quiet space here, but then we go on, in great detail and an oddly settled feeling. We go on for a very long time, most of the night, till Stone falls asleep, arguing about the color of the bedroom.

I'm going to wake him now. There is a new line of light out there and I know he doesn't want to miss any sunrise.

October 17, 1995

Sometimes it just falls apart. All that bravery, all that savor-life, positive stuff. Who could keep it up in the face of the reality forced in our faces? For some reason I woke up haunted by the memory of the man at the park concert. The one that sent Stone running, and me running after him.

Weeks ago. Why is it so sharp for me today? They are playing (amazingly) the Prokofieff "Romeo and Juliet." Wonderful, yearning, angular music with off-center harmonies I love. Stone, who fell asleep at a park concert last year, is listening carefully, but all of a sudden I feel him shake against me. He gets up and walks away.

I find him under a tree, trying to be alone, but I can't let him. I'd seen the man, too. One of a couple. (I refuse to call them anything else, the devotion is so clear.) His partner helps him into the lawn chair, puts an afghan over his knees. He is so thin and wasted that his shirt is huge on him. His skin hangs loosely on his frame, which, where it is exposed, looks like an anatomy lesson. In the dim park lights he looks almost translucent, like shiny, thin wax. No wonder the world doesn't want to look.

Stone is shaking, repelled, terrified. He wants me to go away. Refuses to get like that. He doesn't say, but I know he fears I'll feel

153

the revulsion he feels and hates himself for. Prays it will be fast, instead. We hold each other and try to stay with the music.

But sometimes I can't. Sometimes I wake up in the morning and would give anything to have my mother and father come through the door and hold me and let me cry.

October 18, 1995

Weather forecast: clear tonight, no chance of showers, high 64, low 56. We've been waiting for the right kind of shooting-star night, and I think this may be it.

Stone's been spending his time seeing everyone who contributed to the book, trying to say thank you and, I think, trying to imprint their faces. There hasn't been a whole lot of change in his vision but inevitably there will be, soon. I've inquired about talking books for him, but I'm not going to mention this yet. He's still reading up a storm.

The other day he picked up "A Tale of Two Cities" and read out loud, "It was the best of times; it was the worst of times," and said, "Sounds like us, huh, babe?"

Sometimes I play Future by myself, in my head, getting Stone his G.E.D. and into college, and pretty soon we are discussing literature . . . I suppose Yale is unrealistic, not that he's not smart enough, because he is, but because of his somewhat blemished past.

You are stupid, Yale. It has made him the miracle he is. Your loss. Bard, maybe? I hear they're good with underachievers. Which Stone no longer is. He is a leaping, glorious achiever of more in a few months than most people manage in a long life.

Sometimes I am so washed over with the love of him I feel weak. (The way I used to get when I imagined him without a shirt.) And even though there is something terrifying underneath, it fills me with amazement and gratitude that I know him. That I will always know him, no matter . . . black water. Bungee pull: have to get to the Foundation office and save the world. (Easier.)

154

In the night

So much time, the two of us, staring at the sky recently. We lie there in the middle of the meadow in Elmwood Park, zipped in the same double sleeping bag, and wait.

Stone is worried about the boy Anna is seeing. Lackluster. No credentials. No visible ambition. But, I point out, the good sense to be seeing our daughter, who could use a little loosening up. We decide to give him a break.

I realize it's all the same—this question of time. The whole line of a life that feels like it goes from here to there but is more like one of those dots we are looking at. And that while we feel separate from a given thing or a person—the damp grass under the sleeping bag or the stars overhead, or the individual pressed next to you, looking up—it is all part of the same thing. God, nature, universe, whatever. And it doesn't die.

We waited awhile longer and finally saw what we came for: a star blazing a little brighter than the rest of them, arching across the sky fast and disappearing.

October 19, 1995

Seizure. I meet them in the E.R. Uncle Mac has Stone's blood down the front of him. Felicia says when Stone went down Mac grabbed a bar towel and tried to stop it gushing from his head, while Stone's body jerked and trembled. Mac knew what to do, did what he could while she called 911. She is afraid about the blood and so am I, but Mac doesn't seem to be thinking about it. He's holding my hand, being here.

Stone is conscious, furious, unable to move his whole right side now, yelling slurred to Alan to give him something and end this goddam thing, get it over with.

I didn't know what to pray for. I don't now.

CAT scan suggests toxoplasmosis. Stone doesn't care what it is. Make it stop—the whole thing—him—for good. (Alan, don't, please. Fix it. Can't you fix it for now? I'm not ready.) Alan calm, suspects reaction to foscarnet caused the seizure. Toxo common, treatable, meds. Puts Stone on steroids, sure his brain functions will come back. Stone doesn't care. How much more can he take? Shouts how much can _she_? (He means me.)

155

October 20, 1995

Improvement. Stone can sit up, raise his right hand a little, flex the toes of his right foot. Then all of a sudden goes rigid again.

Another seizure. Alan is not alarmed, says the medication takes time. Stone despondent, but I know, if he can improve just a little, I can raise his spirits.

God, am I being hideously selfish to want him to get better? I know he can't, ultimately, but enough better to stay for a while. We have learned the trick of living in the now. Please give us more of it.

October 21, 1995

Better. He is definitely better. He can move, he can speak distinctly. His right side is weak, but I can tell it's improving. He could have a lot more time. I think he's beginning to want it again.

October 22, 1995

It isn't Stone there. Not Stone talking. It is the drug that is suddenly snarling and venomous in that hospital bed. I have seen Stone angry, sometimes even at me. It is straight and clear and unrepressed. But I have never seen him mean. Never this nasty, never this cruel. I'm not seeing him now. It's the drug.

For the first time it is hard to stay with him. Somebody different behind his eyes. Somebody who explodes and curses, reverts to street talk, is viciously sarcastic, impatient, demanding, everything Stone has never been. And isn't now. It's the drug.

We all have all the programs in our brains, right? The circuits for nice and loving and anything else in the range of human behavior, right down to mean and nasty. The circuits we use are chosen by genetics and conditioning. Right now, the drugs have garbled Stone's circuits. He is not making his own choices.

So there is no point in being all hurt and crushed by it. It's nothing personal. He's democratically rotten to the nurses, to Sonny (who understands, is unflappable), to anyone else in his range. He doesn't need an exorcist. It's the drugs.

There's no point in being hurt by it, but God, it hurts a lot.

October 23, 1995

Alan suspects it may not be toxo after all. What, then? He's not saying. First rule it out. Toxo antibody test.

Stone woke up from a nap, turned and looked at me, and turned his head away. I expected him to say something awful but he didn't. When he turned back his face was wet and all he said was "I'm sorry." Then he asked for Alan and begged him to take him off this stuff.

October 24, 1995

The toxo test was negative. Alan did as Stone asked and took him off the steroids. He's himself again, but very down. I can say it here: so am I. If it isn't toxo, what is it?

Alan ordered a brain biopsy. Oh, God.

October 25, 1995

Raised voices in a hospital corridor. (Unsuitable. Inappropriate.) Is someone angry that someone is dying? I glance at Stone, who's dozing and doesn't wake from the noise, and go to look outside. I see Tony Jones, red-faced, furious, tongue-lashing a young doctor who's swallowing a lot but not saying much, looks alarmed and what . . . a little ashamed? I can't hear what they're saying until Tony stalks off calling over his shoulder, "Fine. I'll handle it myself!" and walks past without seeing me.

Later Alan told me: the resident neurosurgeon (and may he burn) didn't want to do the biopsy. Reason: Stone's disease is advanced; why expose the O.R. team to risk?

October 26, 1995

In an attempt, I think, to control something, Stone asked me to bring him some hairclippers and gave himself a slightly demented haircut, shearing it, in about two minutes, to maybe one inch all over his head. After the initial shock, I think it looks kind of sweet. I kept a lock.

October 27, 1995
General Hospital

When they'd prepped Stone for the procedure and we were waiting to take him down, I asked him how he felt. Scared, he said. (Of a needle in his brain, or more?) So am I, I told him. At least we haven't started lying to each other.

Later

Stone hasn't regained consciousness yet, but Tony said the biopsy went smoothly. Now we wait to hear. What? Whatever we hear, the end's the same.

Why do we need to know? So we can start a countdown? No, maybe because there will be choices. Those famous options.

October 30, 1995

The results have been tallied and the winner is . . . AIDS. Diagnosis: lymphoma. Options: radiation, chemotherapy, or sooner death. And the winner is . . . the contestant has chosen . . . sooner death.

Old rage rising and choking me. I want to kill. Yes, me, Robin. I want to kill everyone who can't help, everyone who has a life, everyone who wasn't as stupid as we were, everyone who hasn't found a cure, everyone who wears those smug red ribbons, and everyone who doesn't.

Stone is much calmer. I suppose there's something in knowing, after not knowing all these months, how it will come. Even in making a choice. No thank you to having my head zapped, no thank you to spending my last days throwing up.

Hell, there are still enough unknowns to keep it interesting, right? Like how long? Will it creep or gallop?

I'm sorry, I'm sorry. This isn't like me, all meanness and sarcasm. It's the drug. The drug of hopelessness. I step from anger to numbness. I don't dare feel what's in between.

November 1, 1995

"It is time to consider a hospice."

Hospice . . . hissing word. Dictionary: "A shelter or lodging for travelers." From the Latin, hospitium, hospitality.

Where is Stone traveling? I wish I knew, in my heart, for sure. I had these things straight in my head when I took my First Communion. (Grandma Fil on the aisle, midway, tears pouring down, I pass her transfixed on my way to thorough Goodness.)

Since then, lots of questions. How? Where? Where is the soul stored? What is its means of transportation? Who will provide it hospitality? Stone wonders—if there's a heaven would anyone who qualifies be anyone he'd really like?

But between now and then and wherever: hospice. A kind place where he can hang out with other travelers.

ABSOLUTELY NOT. Sonny Corinthos has spoken.

He has made Stone a home; what's a home for?

I have, stumblingly, tried to tell Sonny how much I love him.

November 4, 1995

I spend all the time that Stone will let me with him at Sonny's. Still he insists I go into the office. Maybe he needs the space, or thinks I do. I need to let him breathe while he still has the option. Keesha has kindly figured out a lot of "dumb" work for me to do. I wouldn't be surprised if she doesn't do it all over again every day when I leave.

Stone has always teased me about being small, but I point out isn't it fine that I can stay a long time in his lap without undue strain. He can still laugh. Actually we laugh a lot. We replay our relationship. I read him parts of this diary, some of which make me blush, but he might as well know.

He loves the image of him unwrapping me like a present. He says that's right. I am the best gift he ever had, not just that way but every way. Likewise, I say, I'm sure.

November 6, 1995

In the night (I don't sleep at home anymore; Mac makes no objection) we play endless games of Future, Stone almost obses-sive about it, wanting to get every detail, jumping back and forth in time, picking the house (in the city, maybe Charles Street, some-thing like Luke and Laura's, only he would see it got painted); the car(s)—a van for camping and something low and red and sharp; careers for the kids (though ultimately, it is up to them).

I see him very clearly, up on a ladder scraping peeling paint off; in the yard, pushing Sonny-Mac and Anna with alternate hands, on the swings, the baby in one of the those windup types nearby. I come out with sunscreen for all of them. I see him giving orders backstage at a concert, as confident as Lois.

He sees me studying hard, all the time. No fair, I say. How come you get all the fun things? Mr. Mom, he says, so you can finish school. I haven't finished school yet? Med school. Med school??? Med school. Actually, if Mark's been born, you're a resident by now. (Mark? I just like the name.) A resident. What's my specialty? (Not a beat:) Research. You're going to find a cure. I stare. If anyone can do it, babe, you can.

I see us still making love, with gray hair and unbeautiful bodies.

November 7, 1995

Stone sleeps a lot but only in short stints. Sonny and I take turns being with him in the night. Not that he needs us. He can manage to die without us. We need him. We need to be there.

Sometimes I look at him the way Felicia used to go in and look at Georgie when she was sleeping. Sometimes she'd have to look very closely to be sure she was breathing, or touch her to make her stir. Babies sleep so still.

November 9, 1995

Dear Mac. (I mean it.) Insisted Sonny and I get some serious rest. Did we want Stone's last look at us to be with bags under our eyes? Academic, since Stone's vision is failing daily, but we realize we're both strung out and that may be communicating too, so we allow Mac to spell us for a full night's sleep.

In the morning I stand in the door quietly. Stone, beautiful Stone, is sleeping, and my uncle, in the chair next to his bed, is looking down at him with an expression that can only be seen as love. Thank you, God. Thank you.

November 10, 1995

Stone says it won't be long. How does he know? There is a feeling inside him, he says, some kind of motion . . . like skating, or sailing, slowly, smooth, no effort. A pain shoots through me I almost can't stand, quickly numbs itself.

Will you do something for me, Robin? Anything. Get tested. It's not time yet—I'm sure I'm fine. I'd like to know, before. Okay, sure. I'm not worried. That I can do.

November 11, 1995

How do you understand dying?

> *die (1) v. died, dying 1. to cease living. 2. to lose force or vitality. 3. to cease existing 4. (informal) to desire greatly. Synonyms: die, decease, depart, expire, go, pass away, perish, succumb*
> *die (2) n. l. pl. dies. A device that shapes materials by stamping, cutting or punching. 2. pl. dice. One of a pair of dice.*

Which raises the questions: 1. What is the difference between living and existing? (I get the feeling I'm about to find out.) 2. How do we shape each other, by dying? 3. What happens to the other one of the pair?

November 15, 1995

It can't be. It just can't be.

It's positive. It's It. I'm <u>positive</u>. I'm HIV. Positive. Me, Robin Scorpio. Can't be. Has to be a mistake. <u>Has</u> to be. Please, no, please, no, please, God. Can't. It can't be because I'm Robin Scorpio, so smart, so sure, so excellent. Not her. Not me. I don't feel any different. I don't look any different. (Neither did Stone; even now he doesn't much.) Now if I cut my finger people will have to run. Rubber gloves. How can I tell him? Oh, God, don't make me do that to him. Why couldn't it have waited?

If it had to come, why couldn't it wait until after he goes?

Positive. Think positive. Say what you said to Stone: it could be years. In this case, years and years, while millions of dollars get poured into finding a cure. I could have a life. I can have a life. Think well. Be well. Do the right thing. I have to talk to someone, but I don't know who.

The virus is in there, sharpening its teeth.

Later

Went to Kevin. What should I do? Should I tell Stone? He's the one who wanted to know. How can I? I certainly can't tell Mac. Not while Stone is alive. Kevin doesn't know; my decision. Why doesn't he? He's a doctor of the mind. He should have a direction, point me right. I need guidance. He's not refusing. He really doesn't know. Usually he's for truth. Almost always. Here…he's not sure. Kevin Collins, unsure.

Think it over. My disease; my decision. Think about Mac, too. He and Stone have made such progress. What's the point? Stone will be dead.

Mac won't be. Closure. There's plenty of closure coming. For me, too. Go think, Robin. But I had just learned not to. I am afraid. I am so afraid. Afraid to tell. Afraid to die.

Later

I am afraid to tell Mac, not just because of Stone, but because I can't bear to see his pain. To see all his worrying come true for him. And his guilt. He'll blame himself, and he'll hate himself and he doesn't deserve that. Like I don't deserve to die, and neither does Stone.

But if I don't tell him I will have to go back to lying, and I haven't had to do that in a long time. Also, Kevin pointed out that if Mac can have some "closure" with Stone it may relieve them both. Help Mac "down the line." (And he may be alone there.)

Can I trust Uncle Mac not to hurt Stone over this? I think I need to. I'm going to have to trust that Uncle Mac has finally learned to love Stone, and that love is not easily taken back.

Later, Sonny's

Stone in and out of sleep. He seems a little confused, forgetful. Has not asked. Now is not the time, anyway. I have a little time to think. It's so hard: the idea of hurting Stone is awful, but the idea of his dying with that lie between us . . .

I'm going to tell Mac and I'm going to ask his advice. It's been so long since I've done that, he'll probably die of the shock. (How easily, how casually we use that word.)

November 17, 1995

It all went across Mac's face: horror, grief, anger, despair, and finally a fierce love that had nowhere to go but hope. There's time for me that there wasn't for Stone. Stone's disease took hold while he was alone and no one cared, when he didn't have a clue how to take care of himself. I have All the Advantages. Love, care, and time. I have him and he will not let me down.

He didn't let me down about Stone, either. He thinks I should tell him, and he's promised to help with what happens.

I still don't know. Stone is perfectly lucid at times and confused at others. The lymphoma, Tony says. He seems to remember clearly, then forgets, then remembers again. I wish I could tell him and then have him forget right away.

November 20, 1995

Stone seems much clearer, but very weak. I have to do this. God help me and help him.

November 21, 1995

He said nothing. Just stared. He couldn't speak. The most awful look I'd ever seen on his face—the most pain. He turned his face away. A small sound like the groan of an animal. An echo of the night he ran away, bleeding.

I turned his face back, made him look in my eyes. Look at me, listen to me: you did not do this. It happened. It happened to us. A mistake was made, by both of us. Terrible mistakes get made. Awful things happen to people, randomly. I do not blame you. I have it. It is a fact, and I will live with it.

Don't die, Robin. Don't die. His eyes close; he can't look at me anymore, even though all he sees is light and shadow.

I don't plan to die. I will do my best not to, for a long time. I've learned a lot. I'll learn more. Time is on my side.

Later

It was Mac who seemed to reach him. I don't know what he said. Forgiveness? Absolution? If there is no blame, why would it be needed? I guess we all need it.

Stone looks peaceful now. Closure.

November 27, 1995

Very soon. Any day, any hour, any minute. Stone is fragile. Can't see much, but still looks out the window, and I tell him what's there: the city, the lake, light coming off it. He's sorry we never got to the seashore, to swim with the dolphins. We can, I say. If we can have a house and children we can certainly have dolphins. In fact, I see a school of them, out there in the lake. He reminds me dolphins are sea creatures. I don't care, there they are, just off shore.

I take his hand and we plunge into the water. From one lesson he has become a strong swimmer. He moves ahead of me, turns back and laughs. I strain and catch up. The dolphins seem to be waiting for us. We swim beside them. A pair invites us to mount. We ride them briefly, joyfully, then plunge back into the water and keep swimming, together, way out beyond them.

November 29, 1995

Brenda and Sonny by his chair. He knows they are not togeth-er yet, but he believes they will be.

Stone sleeps, wakes, we wait. When he's awake we laugh about everything we can think of: the night of the popcorn, the night of the bear, lost Lollapalooza, skunked, and tomato juice.

Some of it Brenda and Sonny have never heard, and love. Robin and Stone lore. Stone is weak but has enough strength to laugh, then is quiet. Everything is quiet. He asks me to move close to the window, move close to the light.

I see you, he says. And I know he does.

Something moves out of him and goes away.

I kiss his eyes closed.

Good-bye, my love. God bless. God keep.

DEAR ROBIN,

THIS IS THE FIRST LETER I EVER WROTE. ITS rite THAT IT IS TO YOU, bechuse WITHOUT YOU, I wuldnT be ABlE TO DO THIS MUCH. I am whriTing iT NOW bechuse I THINK prety SOON I wonT be ABLE TO SEE TO DO iT.

I LOVE YOU. I WILL NOT SAY GOODby TO YOU. I DO NOT KNOW where I am GOING buT I BELEVE IT IS TO SOME PLACE AND I WILL GO ON LOVING YOU FROM THERE ALWAYS.

IF I DID NOT KNOW YOU I WULD NOT MIND DYING, becaus I LOVE YOU I DO NOT WANT TO LEVE MY life, I JUST WANT TO HOLD YOU AND LOOK AT YOU AND LISTEN TO YOU, and THIS SEEMS SO butiful TO me AND SO good THAT iT HUrTS, AND THERe IS PAIN IN MY CHEST, and IT IS MY HEART.

I WANT YOUR life TO BE long AND Full OF LOVE becaus THEN You will BE HAPPY.

I WANT YOU TO HAVE YEARS TO GIVE THE WORLD ~~THAT~~ WHAT YOU GAVE ME becaus iT will be A BETTER place lIKE I AM beTer becaus you love Me. AND THEN WHERE ever iT IS I will See YOU aGAIN.

Stone

December 1, 1995

Sonny gave me this today before Stone's memorial service. He found it in Stone's top bureau drawer. On the envelope was printed "Plese give to Robin."

Selections from
Stone's Memory Book

Dear Stone,

You're probably wondering why I'm writing this instead of simply saying what I have to say to your face. But this isn't easy for me, and I'm afraid if I try to explain it, I'll mess up. I do that sometimes.

Something happened to me today at the AIDS walk that took me by surprise. A mirror was held up, and I saw myself in it, and I didn't like what I saw. That woman represented the most narrow-minded, bigoted, and prejudiced among us. Yet she was so convinced of her own superiority. When I saw how you handled her, and I recognized how wrong she was about you and AIDS and the way people react out of ignorance, I knew I had some major soul-searching to do.

To begin with, I owe you a personal apology for some of the things I've said and done. I also owe you a debt of gratitude for opening my eyes. Things are not what they seem, or what we wish them to be. Neither are people. It's a lesson I'm learning late, but one I won't forget. And if there's one thing I might do to make up for my past behavior, it's to make you this solemn promise: to recognize and move beyond my own prejudices and to not be so quick to rush to judgment.

You're very strong, Stone. You proved that today when you stood up for yourself. But should you ever find you need someone to stand up with you, you know where to find me.

Respectfully yours,

Alan Quartermiane, Jr.

Dear Stone,

This song is dedicated to you on my album.   And
when I sing it in concert, I will sing it for
you.

Your friend,

Miguel

Power to Believe

There's a face here in the mirror
One I hardly recognize
The fire's burning low
Behind those tired eyes
Do you believe that love
Can heal a broken dream

And faith can move a mountain
Till it melts into the sea?

There's just one thing I want just one thing I need
You to stand beside me and the power to believe

Time moves in the shadows
A clock with missing hands
And your silence means more to me
Than words ever can
Is there a heaven waiting
On the other side?
Or do we find heaven
Just by looking here inside?

There's just one thing I want just one thing I need
You to stand beside me and the power to believe

Do you believe that love
Can heal a broken dream
And faith can move a mountain
Till it melts into the sea?

Here's just one thing I want just one thing I need
You to stand beside me and the power to believe
The power to believe

Dear Stone,

My parents have taught me a lot of things they say are important about getting along with people.

When I think of two of them in particular, and then think of you, I know my parents are right. At least about this.

My mother says treat everybody the way you would like them to treat you. My father says listen. Just shut up and listen to what the other guy is trying to tell you. You know how to do both of these things, and it makes you a really good friend. And I just wanted to tell you that.

Sincerely,

Lucky

Felicia Jones

Dear Stone,

In many ways, Robin has been my daughter. In all ways, she has been my friend. I have laughed with her and wept for her and worried about her and rejoiced in her, and I've come to understand how deeply and truly she loves you—and how much you love her in return. You both grew up so quickly, and you continue to grow so bravely. I admire you, and I celebrate you both.

With love,

Felicia

Dear Stone,

A couple of hours ago, I sat down at my desk to try to put on paper from Bobbie and me some good wishes for you and a few of the thoughts we've had about the courage with which you've handled one bad break after another. Everything I wrote sounded pretty much like a bad message from a greeting card. So I'm sitting here surrounded by little balls of scrunched-up paper, and Lucas comes in and asks what I'm doing. I try to explain. He listens and goes away and comes back in twenty minutes or so with the attached. In case it isn't perfectly obvious....

The large stick figure with the big smile is you. The object over your head with what appears to be many wavy arms is the sun, which is shining on you. To your right is a tree, and on a branch is a bird, which is singing to you. That's a musical note over his head. The smiling faces with sort of hairy heads at your feet are flowers, which your friends planted for you. And best of all, the figure next to you is Robin. Contrary to first impression, that is not a sword she is pointing at you; it's an ice cream cone. The specks are chocolate sprinkles.

I figure Bobbie and I can't improve on these sentiments.

With love from

Lucas
Bobbie
Tony

172

Brenda Barrett

Stone,

On the docks, with the first ice cream cones of
summer, you with three scoops melting faster than
you could keep up with, vanilla ice cream to your
elbows, Robin laughing so hard she dropped hers
into her lap....You giving Ruby awful grief over a
raisin in your oatmeal which you insisted was a fly,
and finally giving in, "Okay. Okay, Ruby; it's a
raisin. But it's a raisin with six legs." Customers
gagging and signalling for checks....When the base-
ball strike was over, walking down the street in
front of the Port Charles Hotel, you and Sonny
singing "Take Me Out to the Ballgame" in two different keys, really the most lame and hideous and
loud presentation of that song I've ever heard, and
the doorman asking me to move you along....Small
events, Stone, brief, funny, to whom are they
important now? To me. Who will remember them
and all the others like them? I will. Ordinary
moments of shared joy. You've taught me to take
none of them for granted, and I won't, not ever
again. How can I thank you for giving me that?

Love,

Brenda

Dear Stone,

Sigmund asked me to give this to you.
With love from him and

Lucy

I bet that you are thunderstruck
To read doggerel from a duck.
But Lucy's splendid waterfowl
Is wiser than the wisest owl,
More clever far than jay or crow:
I'll quack you up with what I know.
And what this poem means to tell
Is: Stone, I think that you are swell.

Very truly yours,

Sigmund

Dear Stone,

Lois and I agreed we would write this to you together. I am sitting at the computer and she is leaning over the back of my chair and talking non-stop into my ear, a phenomenon with which I know you are familiar, and which is endearing when you love her, but it means I'm having a little difficulty collecting my own thoughts, so this won't be as elegant as I'd like it to be.

Stone, it's Lois now. In this case, I think we should forget elegant and just go for the heart of the matter, which is we both feel you are such a gift to us. I always wanted a younger brother, because older brothers think they know it all, and you are the younger brother of my heart because we share so many interests and ambitions and I love you very, very much.

It's Ned again. This means you're kind of my brother-in-law, a great arrangement because I think you're as classy an act as my wife, and more than that I can't say about anyone.

And when the history of L&B Records—Lois here again—is written, there will be a special chapter on Stone and what he has meant to the company and all of us.

We love you.

Lois & Ned

Luke Spencer

Dear Stone,

My first impression was that you were a screw-up. This was also the subject of my first real argument with Corinthos. I did, however, from the start appreciate your style in getting in Mac's face. Regrettably for you, it reminded me of me at your age.

My second impression was that Corinthos was right; I was wrong. This happens occasionally, if infrequently. But there it was: you had potential.

My current impression is that you are a man whom I would be damn grateful to have at my side or guarding my back in perilous times. I wish my friend Robert Scorpio could have known you. I'm glad I do.

Luke

Dear Stone,

Shortly after you came into Robin's life and mine, I began grinding my teeth at night. Rather than walk around with an aching jaw and loose molars, I trained myself to wake up when I started to grind, and subsequently spent a lot of time lying in the dark and thinking about the kind of guy I'd choose for Robin if I had any choice in the matter, which I clearly didn't.

He would think of her before himself. He would commit himself to loving her, cherishing her, understanding her. He would respect her intellectual gifts. He would have something unique and valuable coming from his own experience to offer her in exchange for what she brought to him. He would be unconventional, but understand the social contract. He would have a wide diversity of friends. He would be loyal to them. He would have humor. He would have courage.

And then I realized the guy I would choose for Robin sounded more and more like you.

I forgot one thing. He would think I am incredibly smart and indescribably cool. Okay. We can work on that.

Mac

Stone, my man—

You just went off to bed and left me here with BB and Lucille working on "The Midnight Blues" and I figure it's a good time to try and do what Robin asked.

She said remember things that would make you laugh. What puts me away is how you can laugh in the middle of all this. How you can take stuff that nearly stops me from breathing when I think about it and cut it down to size with one of those gross, black comments you're getting so good at....In a way, with all respect to Robin, it feels presumptuous to try to make you laugh about anything.

Then I think about times like you mad at me for leaving the Jag out in the parking lot at 4:00 A.M. and going down in your undershorts and sneakers to put it in the garage not knowing the temperature had dropped thirty degrees and locking yourself out and yelling under my window till I came out of a long hot shower and heard you and went to let you in. Or the time you were going to prove to me that any fool can cook and freaked when the lobsters tried to climb out of the pot. Or when instead of three cloves of garlic you tossed three heads of garlic (unpeeled) into the marinara sauce. And then ate it, because no way were you going to admit it was foul....I remember other things, not funny, that will be with me for the rest of my life. The first time I saw you with the other kids under the viaduct by the train yards, standing over the oil drum fire, the light on your face and your teeth chattering while you pretended you weren't freezing your tail off in a blue jean jacket with the wind coming off the lake, and nobody had a clue who ripped off my car radio....

I could go on with this all night, but that's not the point. The idea is we've shared a lot of stuff and I've learned a hell of a lot more from you than you have from me, and I'm real grateful for that. And I love you, man.

Sonny

AIDS Organizations

To learn more about AIDS, about services and support available to people who are HIV positive, and about ways to contribute your time, money, or other resources, consult the following list.

Adolescent Risk Evaluation Program
Montefiore Medical Center
111 E. 210 Street
Bronx, NY 10467
718-882-0023
Provides treatment and education for adolescents at risk for or living with AIDS.

AIDS and Adolescents Network of New York
121 Sixth Avenue, 6th Floor
New York, NY 10013
212-925-6675
Advocates for changes in public policy affecting young people and AIDS; provides education resources and referrals, focusing on youth with HIV/AIDS.

AIDS and Cancer Research Foundation
8306 Wilshire Blvd., Suite 1800
Beverly Hills, CA 90211
1-800-373-4572 Voice
213-655-1804 FAX
Provides educational and prevention information about AIDS; raises public awareness and promotes research.

AIDS Clinical Trials Information Service (ACTIS)
Hours of operation: 9 A.M.–7 P.M. Eastern time
1-800-TRIALS-A (874-2572) Voice (English and Spanish)
1-800-243-7012 TTY/TDD
301-217-0023 International
301-738-6616 FAX
Provides current information on federally and privately sponsored clinical trials (including printouts from a custom search of the databases) to HIV-positive individuals and exposed healthcare workers.

AIDS National Interfaith Network
110 Maryland Avenue NE, Suite 504
Washington, DC 20002
202-546-0807 Voice   202-546-5103 FAX
Provides referrals to appropriate local faith resources for HIV positive individuals and their loved ones, regardless of religion.

AIDS Treatment Data Network
611 Broadway, Room 613
New York, NY 10012
1-800-734-7104 Hotline
Provides treatment information (including database of clinical trials) and referrals (for such things as medical care, acupuncture, approved alternative treatments, and caregivers) to HIV-positive individuals.

American Foundation for AIDS Research (AMFAR)
733 Third Avenue, 12th Floor
New York, NY 10017
212-682-7440 Voice
Funds biomedical and clinical research dedicated to finding a cure for AIDS; publishes an AIDS treatment directory of clinical trials that is updated twice yearly and available by phone order; co-founded in 1985 by Elizabeth Taylor.

Centers for Disease Control National AIDS Hotline
1-800-342-AIDS (2437) Voice
1-800-243-7889 TDD Monday–Friday, 10 A.M.–10 P.M. Eastern time
1-800-344-7432 Voice (Spanish) 8 A.M.–2 A.M. Eastern time
Provides answers to basic questions about AIDS and referrals for nformation on testing means of transmission, prevention, treatment, and other AIDS-related issues.

Gay Men's Health Crisis, Inc.
129 West 20 Street New York, NY 10011
212-807-7660 Voice (English and Spanish)
212-807-6655 Hotline
Provides counseling, ombudsmanship, and information on recreation opportunities and legal and financial aid to any HIV-positive individual; advocates for public awareness and changes in public policy.

179

HIV/AIDS Treatment Information Service
(ATIS)
Hours of operation: 9 A.M. - 7 P.M.
Eastern time
1-800-HIV-0440 (448-0440) Voice
(English and Spanish)
Provides information on federally approved
treatments for HIV infection and AIDS.

Impact AIDS, Inc.
3692–18th Street
San Francisco, CA 94110
415-861-3397 Voice
415-863-AIDS (2437) Hotline for specific
information
415-621-3951 FAX
Distributes educational material produced by
the San Francisco AIDS Foundation.

The Magic Johnson Foundation
1888 Century Park East, Suite 310
Los Angeles, CA 90067
310-785-0201 Voice
Raises funds for AIDS-related causes.

The Names Project Foundation
(sponsor of the AIDS Memorial Quilt)
310 Townsend, Suite 310
San Francisco, CA 94107
415-882-5500 Voice   415-882-6200 FAX
Coordinates creation and display of the AIDS
Memorial Quilt, which commemorates those
who have died from AIDS and reminds the
public of the enormity and personal impact
of the disease.

National AIDS Fund
1400 I Street NW, Suite 1220
Washington, DC 20005
202-408-4848 Voice
Provides information on AIDS education and
prevention programs.

National Association of People with AIDS
(NAPWA)
1413 K Street NW
Washington, DC 20005
202-898-0414 Voice   202-789-2222 FAX
(must have touch-tone phone)
Provides information regarding AIDS
education, litigation, research, and referrals;
operates mail-order pharmacy; conducts

lobbying and outreach, including the Spiro
Coalition of Speakers; provides fax-on-
demand information for HIV-positive
individuals and their caregivers.

National Leadership Coalition on AIDS
1730 M Street NW, Suite 905
Washington, DC 20036
202-429-0930 Voice
Provides counseling and information
regarding AIDS in the work-place.

Pediatric AIDS Foundation
1311 Colorado Avenue
Santa Monica, CA 90404
310-395-9051 Voice
Exclusively funds research dedicated to AIDS
and HIV infection in children, including
research to find a cure, to develop new
treatments, and to block maternal fetal
transmission of the HIV virus.

Project Inform Treatment
1965 Market Street, Suite 220
San Francisco, CA 94103
10 A.M.–4 P.M. West Coast time
1-800-334-7422 CA Hotline
1-800-822-7422 National Hotline
Provides referral for AIDS and HIV treatment
information; offers basic treatment packet by
phone order; advocates for policy changes
with drug agencies and government.

Ryan White Foundation
1717 West 86 Street,
Suite 220 Indianapolis, IN 46260
1-800-444-RYAN (7926) Voice
Works to increase public awareness of AIDS
and acceptance of individuals, especially
teens, with AIDS; provides information, support, counseling, and financial assistance
to HIV-positive teens and their families.